LEARNING '
TRUST HER MATES

Lost in Space 2

Marla Monroe

MENAGE EVERLASTING

Siren Publishing, Inc.
www.SirenPublishing.com

A SIREN PUBLISHING BOOK
IMPRINT: Ménage Everlasting

LEARNING TO TRUST HER MATES
Copyright © 2016 by Marla Monroe

ISBN: 978-1-68295-237-5

First Printing: March 2016

Cover design by Les Byerley
All art and logo copyright © 2016 by Siren Publishing, Inc.

ALL RIGHTS RESERVED: This literary work may not be reproduced or transmitted in any form or by any means, including electronic or photographic reproduction, in whole or in part, without express written permission.

All characters and events in this book are fictitious. Any resemblance to actual persons living or dead is strictly coincidental.

Printed in the U.S.A.

PUBLISHER
Siren Publishing, Inc.
www.SirenPublishing.com

LEARNING TO TRUST HER MATES

Lost in Space 2

MARLA MONROE

Copyright © 2016

Chapter One

"You are uncomfortable around me, Caro. Why? Have I frightened you or insulted you in some way?" Gressen cocked his head to one side as he stared at the most beautiful creature he'd ever seen.

"No! No. I'm just not used to everything yet. It's only been two months. You and Sabin have been nothing but kind to me." Caro's wide eyes gave him the reassurance he needed that she was being truthful.

If it weren't for the translators being developed so that all life forms could communicate, no matter their language, he might not have the chance to gain favor with a female of such statue. Her smiles, though rare, brought warmth to him and his brother's cold world. Without communication, none of the thousands and thousands of different species would have ever been able to trade, band together for safety, or understand the ways of their enemies.

Now the tiny implanted unit smoothed the way for his kind to court these human females in hopes they would agree to be their mates.

"We would never knowingly do these things to you. You are our guest and a female. To us, you are a rare treat with your smiles and bright eyes. We have enjoyed your presence in our home." Gressen watched as the pretty female looked everywhere but at him.

It saddened him that she didn't seem to be forming a bond with him or his brother, Sabin. He'd hoped she would eventually agree to be their mate, but hope was quickly fading for them. Should he offer to allow her to move to another home, or would she feel rejected? He wasn't sure what the best course of action would be. He needed to discuss it with Sabin.

"Gressen, I love your home and have really learned so much from you and your brother. It's great to be so close to Della as well. We can talk about everything we are learning, and help each other with some of the things we might not understand." She walked across the room until she was only a few feet away from where he stood. "I'm sorry if I appear ungrateful. I honestly don't mean to."

"No. I did not mean to insinuate that, my lovely flower. I'm just worried that we are doing something that makes you nervous of us or uncomfortable in our home. There are still so many things and customs we don't know about each other and, um, stepping on fingers is going to occur."

The sound of her charming laugh tore at his heart. To hear that all the time and to know it was because he'd pleased her gave him the greatest of thrills. He'd copy and repeat whatever caused it if he could only understand what it was.

"Gressen, I think you mean that stepping on toes is bound to happen." She smiled, brightening her normally sad eyes.

"Ah. I understand. I will remember that next time. Thank you, Caro." He curled his fingers into the palms of his hands to keep from reaching out to her.

"Sabin will be home this evening. We were hoping you might feel up to letting us show you some of our city, and take the evening meal in the commons."

"I'd love to see more. It was so pretty when we first arrived, but I was pretty wiped out and only caught a brief look." Caro smiled but it soon faltered. "Is the commons like a restaurant would be back on Earth?"

"I do not believe so. You have many of those where people eat all the time, right?" At her nod he continued. "The commons is the only such place we have. It is a large area where everyone can gather for meals, meetings, and entertainment. It is very rare that everyone is there at the same times. That only happens when there is an important announcement from our council."

"Do you think that maybe Della, Kane, and Veran could come, too?" she asked.

Gressen had anticipated that she would want Vella with her, and had already asked Kane if they might join him and Sabin to take Caro out. He was glad they'd agreed. Though he wanted his sweet Caro flower to feel comfortable with just him and his brother, he understood how difficult this was for a female, especially someone as vulnerable as she appeared to be.

"Of course. I asked Kane, if we decided to go, would they like to join us, and he was sure they would. It will be a treat for their Della as well. She hasn't been yet either."

"Great. We can look like tourists together," she said with another of her rare, sweet smiles.

"Tourists?" He frowned. "I don't believe I know that term. It wasn't one that we heard on the programs."

"It means someone who isn't from an area who is visiting to look around and sight see," she explained.

"Ah," was all he could think to say to that.

"Is there a dress code for going to this commons place? I don't want to wear something that isn't appropriate and embarrass you and Sabin," she said.

"Sweet flower, you would never embarrass us. Females can do no wrong in our world. You are precious and should always be comfortable. There is no, as you say, dress code. The environment for the walk will be slightly cooler than how we keep it here, but once inside the commons, if they have the walls up, it will be more comfortable."

"The walls up? I don't understand," Caro said, her brows furrowing together.

"Hmm, I think you have doors that roll up when you wish to store your transport in the house. I believe it would be similar to that, but much larger." He smiled, sure he'd gotten that correct.

Once again, she giggled and her face transformed into a bright ray of one of their suns. He'd misstated something again. If it made her happy, he wouldn't worry about it. He had no issue with appearing ignorant should it bring her amusement.

"I can tell that I've spoken something incorrectly again." He gave an exaggerated shake of his head and lowered his eyes. "What was my error this time, Caro?"

"I don't mean to laugh, but it's so funny to hear some of the things you come up with. Please, don't be hurt," she said, stepping closer and laying one of her delicate hands on his bare arm.

A thrill trilled across his skin and electrified his heart so that it beat a little faster. To feel her hands on him always, and in intimate ways, had his maleness hardening.

What is it that Kane told me they call the male member? I think it was his coke. No, that is a drink they like. His cock, maybe.

He froze so that maybe she wouldn't think anything of touching him, and leave her hand there a little longer. But the moment she realized what she'd done, Caro dropped her arm and stepped back once again.

"I'm not hurt, Caro. You couldn't harm me if you tried. We are larger and stronger than your males."

"I meant emotionally. I know I couldn't stand a chance against your people. The Levassians are an amazing people with excellent health and appearance. I just meant that I didn't mean to hurt your feelings." Her cheeks grew rosy, as did her neck. Gressen couldn't help but wonder if her skin did that across her chest as well.

He ached to touch her all over. He wanted to see what her breasts would be like. Humans were much softer than Levassians. Even their females, before the Eros scourge wiped them out, didn't have skin as soft as these humans. The virus had attacked only the females of their race, and before taking their lives, it had made them infertile. Though they hadn't been able to prove it, many thought it a virus created to wipe out their entire race.

Gressen clenched his hands in an effort not to reach out and touch her without her permission. The need was so strong to test his theory that her skin would be smooth and soft all over her body. The males of the race were soft as well, but not as much. He had no doubt they would take exception to his observations. They were a prideful species, something his people had slowly cultivated out of their culture many years before Gressen was born.

"We call our transports cars or trucks, and we park them in garages or carports, not actually inside our houses," she explained with twitching lips.

Gressen smiled. "I suppose we did think it a bit odd that you would want such things inside your homes. Now I understand."

"I would love to go with you and Sabin this evening," Caro said out of the blue.

It caught him off guard and he stuttered his answer. "T—that's wonderful. Sabin will be pleased as well."

The sweet Earth female dropped her eyes once more. "I'm going to my room to decide what to wear. I think I'll take a nap so I will be rested for the walk."

"Of course. Our longer days and two suns are still taking a toll on all of your people. Rest is very good for you, Caro. I will check on you before Sabin returns," he told her.

Caro nodded, giving him a shy smile before turning to stroll toward her room between his and Sabin's. The sight of her softly swaying ass gave both his heart and his member, his *cock*, a thrill. There had to be something they could do to make her truly their Caro. It was his fondest dream, and yet, it seemed impossible. Maybe the walk and meeting others of his race would make her feel less uncomfortable. He refused to give up hope.

* * * *

Caro threw herself down on the bed. Why couldn't she relax around Gressen and Sabin? They were so nice to her, and had worked hard to make her comfortable, seeing to her ever need. Her friend Della, was ecstatically happy with her relationship with Veran and Kane. She talked about how amazing it was to have two men treat her like a national treasure, and that the sex was mind blowing. Even though Kane was from Earth, he was of American Indian heritage and a very proud and handsome man. Veran was Levassian and an important member of their security force, or army, or something. He'd fallen for Della almost immediately, and had welcomed Kane without prejudice.

It's just me. All my life men have fawned over me, but it wasn't me they liked. It was my body, or my connections in the industry they wanted. Never me. The real me.

There had been too many times she'd thought she'd finally found someone who loved her, and not her model-like looks, bank account, or contacts. She thought they weren't out to use her, but she'd been wrong. Time after time, men and women had betrayed her and used her for what they'd wanted. She was so afraid it would happen again.

"I know it won't be because of my contacts, since we aren't on Earth anymore, neither is it my money. I don't have any now, and they don't use money. From what Della has told me, they value larger, sturdier women with more meat on their bones, so it isn't going to be my looks that will draw them to me."

Turning over on her back, Caro stared at the metal-like smoothness of the ceiling. She was afraid that the only reason they really wanted her or liked her was because she was a female who could give them children. Once again, she was afraid that Gressen and Sabin would overlook the real her. They wouldn't mean to, but it was bound to happen when she wasn't someone who exerted herself so that she garnered attention. It meant, who she really was got overlooked or ignored.

Caro wasn't a shallow person. She had dreams and aspirations just like anyone else. She'd wanted to somehow make a difference in the world, but wasn't sure how. Now, she had no ideas about the world she found herself in. As far as she could tell, it was a sort of paradise with no real problems in their society. At least Gressen hadn't mentioned any.

They had the wild creature problem, if you ventured out of the city, but nothing that she could possibly help in some way. She needed a cause, or she'd end up being just what she feared, a useless, mentally slow female who just needed a baby on board to feel complete.

It had only been two months, but it felt like a lifetime ago that they'd crashed on the planet of Levasso on their way to planet Omega from Earth. Earth's sun was dying, and, as a result, it was tearing apart their planet and the atmosphere. The increased amount of radiation and other byproducts of the disaster were also causing women to become infertile. As soon as they'd figured that out, they'd sequestered all females who tested positive to still having viable eggs until they could secure another planet that would sustain human life. Fortunately, or unfortunately, depending on how you looked at it, Caro had been one of the few who still had viable eggs. Not only that, but she appeared to be one of the perfect incubators for the little suckers once they were fertilized.

Now, here she was on a very different planet, among people she didn't know. Even Della was new to her, though she felt like they'd known each other a lifetime. She had the unique opportunity to start over where no one knew her, or what she'd been before. Instead of her modeling career defining who she was to others, it was her ability to have children that did so. How would she ever know if it was her that they saw when they looked at her, or her eggs?

Caro liked Gressen and Sabin. They were kind, caring, and seemed to genuinely care if she was okay or not. They were handsome men, though different.

Gressen stood seven feet tall with golden skin that seemed almost metallic in color. He had wide shoulders and was muscular, yet his body yielded when you touched it. She'd always hated to touch any of the hard-as-a-rock body builders she was often paired with for photo shoots. Even their skin felt hard. But Gressen's skin was soft. He moved with an easy grace that someone as tall as he, and most of the Levassians, shouldn't be able to do. His dark green eyes had the Levassians' golden circle around the pupils that made him look so unique. With his deep, resonating voice and soft-spoken words, he was every ounce a male, but with none of the testosterone bleeding aggression the males from Earth had in spades.

His brother, Sabin, was equally soft spoken, though his voice held a slightly higher tone. He was maybe an inch taller than Gressen and had eyes a slightly darker shade of green encircled with gold. His skin held a slightly less shiny gold tent to it, and was a little more muscular. He had long fingers and, as a healer, she imagined that stood him well. Both brothers had bright yellow hair that was pulled back at the nape of their necks. Despite feeling awkward around them, Caro still wanted to release the tie from their hair and see how it fell and what it felt like.

How could she possibly not like them when they made sure it was okay with her first with everything they did? In all likelihood, they were sincere and cared about her as someone who mattered, and not because of what they hoped to gain from her.

Still, that little voice inside of her warned that since they had no females on their planet after the Eros scourge, she was a coveted commodity.

That's not fair. They don't treat me like a piece of property as they had back on Earth. I don't feel used around them, but as a female and able to have children, I'm valuable to them. To have me, a Levassian probably wouldn't care what I looked like or how intelligent or dumb I was, as long as I was female and could give them children.

Why couldn't she put it behind her and start over here without wondering if it was her they liked or her body, or in this case, her eggs? Was she just afraid to take a chance again, or was it that she was afraid that she would be wrong and they did actually like her for who she was inside? Men were usually the ones who had commitment problems, but maybe this time it was her.

No matter how much she obsessed about it, Caro could never put her fears to rest. Somehow, she had to try, or she was going to make herself sick and old at only twenty-eight. She imagined herself with gray hair and a stooped body sitting on a rocking chair in front of one of the domed family homes. Oddly enough, Sabin sat on one side of her and Gressen the other, both rocking and holding her hands.

Chapter Two

"I'm not sure that this is a good idea, brother," Sabin said as he finished straightening his clothes. "She's going to be overwhelmed by the differences in our cultures all at once."

"I disagree. I think it will go a long way in helping her to adjust. Right now, she is insulated from our world, and no doubt feels trapped. That is why I have Della and her mates going with us. They will be able to experience it all together," Gressen said.

"Maybe you are right, but I don't feel she is adjusting to us anyway. I'm not sure she would choose us when she is ready to join a family unit. She will probably want a human male to be at least one of her mates."

"I think she is adjusting to us just fine. Give her some time. This is a huge change in her life." Gressen patted his brother on the shoulder and left him there to finish getting ready.

Sabin really liked Caro. Something about her quiet grace and that amazing smile had him smitten from the beginning. He would like nothing more than to be honored as one of her choices as mate, but held out little hope. He was a lowly healer, even though his brother was one of the elite heads of their security forces.

I am allowing my thoughts to get ahead of things. I don't think she is the least bit attracted to me. Do I want her to feel she has to choose me if she wishes to mate with my brother? I can always step aside and take over one of the other empty family units.

But, that wasn't what he deeply wanted. It would devastate something inside of him to separate their family units and find he was lacking in a female's eyes next to his brother. As a healer, he was valued, but considered weak and unable to protect the city or its inhabitants. None of his people would ever offend him by saying such to him or his brother, but they would know this as it was taught. It already gave him a feeling of unworthiness to claim a mate, so having one turn from him would be the ultimate in humiliation for him.

He was honored and grateful that his brother included him in the family unit, despite his status. It attested to his loyalty and love that he wanted to share a mate with him, but he felt it was unfair to the resplendent female.

"Are you ready, brother? Caro is talking to Della while we assemble." Gressen walked to his doorway but didn't enter.

"I am ready. Be sure to keep close to her so that nothing happens to her," he told his brother.

Gressen rolled his eyes. "We will both keep her safe. You are as capable as I am to protect her, brother."

Sabin disagreed, but kept his thoughts to himself. His brother had always included him in everything, including his early training. Sabin's healing abilities and quick intellect hadn't deterred Gressen from pulling him from his studies to build his strength and talents in that area.

When they entered the joined common area, Caro's splendid laugh with the tinkling notes like music soothed his agitation. She stood in one of the beautiful purple robes prepared for her, talking to her friend, Della. The other woman wore a deep green robed outfit with what looked like blousy pants beneath it. He'd never really seen a female in such, but considering what they'd been wearing when they'd found them, it was an improvement in his eyes.

"I believe we are ready to leave," Gressen said from behind him.

Caro turned toward them, and to Sabin's surprise, her smile became wider and a brilliant, sparkling light danced in her eyes before she dropped them to stare at her feet. It encouraged him that she might hold some fondness for them. Just the sight of that smile had aroused his male member. He wasn't yet able to call it the words Gressen had explained to him.

Cock, what a ridiculous word for the male's sex member. I do not believe it would be acceptable for Caro. She's much too delicate for guttural talk like that.

As they left their unit, Della snuggled between her mates, Kane and Veran, as if the two males made her happier than anything. Desire and a wistful need tightened like a band around his heart. To feel sweet Caro's hand in his would be a torture he'd endure to the ends of their time.

Gressen placed one hand at the small of her back and she didn't protest. His brother looked over her head at him, gave a brief nod, then stared at her arm. It was obvious he wanted him to hold her hand as the others were doing, but Sabin couldn't bring himself to attempt it, only to have her pull from his grasp. Instead, he satisfied himself with lightly gripping her elbow.

Caro looked up into his eyes with a bemused expression, then smiled before dropping her head to watch where she was going. Pleasure coursed through his bloodstream as he savored the warmth it gave him to have witnessed that smile for him alone.

"What do you think of the buildings, Caro?" Della asked, looking over her shoulder to where they followed behind them. "Aren't they beautiful?"

"They are. I love the diversity and all the bright colors. Even the few that have a more pastel look are pretty. I wonder why those aren't as bright?" Caro asked.

"Those are what you might call government buildings. They house our council, our dignitaries who oversee any trade agreements we might have, and those who handle the day-to-day necessities of keeping our city operational," Gressen explained to them.

"What about police departments or jails, or courts?" Kane asked as he looked around them.

"I'm not sure about all of those terms," Gressen said. "Veran? What am I missing?"

"Those are punishment and security forces," Veran explained. "We have no need for those here. I've told you that we are actually very peaceful. Unless we are invaded and attacked, there's no need for our security force. We only keep it always at the ready after what we've been through in the past."

"What do you do if you're not keeping the peace, Gressen?" Caro asked.

Sabin watched as his brother smiled down at her. "I perform other duties after I've trained with my teams. Veran is on my team. We then work at other things afterward."

"Like what?" Della asked her mate.

"Sometimes I help in the fields if it is harvest time. Sometimes I help with repairing our elders' units. We all help out, wherever we are needed. That is what keeps our city going and everyone pleased with their place in life." Veran kissed the top of his mate's head.

"Sabin? Are you busy all day, or do you do other things as well?" Caro asked.

Again, her lovely face was tipped up to look at him. He could have drowned in her light blue eyes. They were as their sky in the youth of their years. Her colorless hair, that held hints of gold in it when it moved the right way, hung down her back, almost to her waist. He'd never seen hair that way, or the darker skin tone that seemed almost bronze but wasn't. Though he was tall, Caro stood just at his shoulder, the perfect height for him to drape his arms around hers, if he had the nerve.

"Um, I manage the health complex, so I'm always busy there. Even if we are not seeing to anyone's needs at the moment. I do have a little extra time, on occasion, and if there is a need that I'm qualified to help with, I do." He hated qualifying his shortcomings, but wasn't going to give her any false information either.

"Qualified? Why wouldn't you be qualified to help with anything? I would think that, as a doctor, um, healer, you'd be more than qualified for anything you wanted to do. I can't even imagine how intelligent you must be," Caro said.

"As a healer, he isn't allowed to do anything that might injure his hands, or any of his abilities to perform his services," Veran said. "He is very valuable to our people."

"I would expect so," Caro said smiling up at him. "My brother wanted to be a doctor, a healer, but there was no money for him to go all eight years it would have taken him to complete his training. Once I started earning money as a model, I supplemented his earnings so that he was finally able to go. Then things began to change and he had to become a nurse instead."

The sight of Caro's sorrow hurt his soul. "What has made you so sad, kitten?"

Her eyes brightened for a moment. "Kitten?"

"I'm sorry. It slipped out. I would never insult you. It is an endearment to us. Uh, the kitten here is a sweet, furry creature that loves to be cuddled and touched. I meant no harm, Caro." Sabin was horrified that he'd let such an intimate word escape his mouth. What would she think of him now?

"That's so sweet. Thank you." She smiled, then ducked her head. "I miss my brother and wonder if he's okay. He was so disappointed that he'd had to stop his studies and was forced into nursing instead. They wanted him for the first mission that went to planet Alpha. Um, our family was blessed, or cursed, however you want to look at it, with extreme intelligence and amazing reproduction capabilities. We were drafted into becoming populaters for the new colonies. I just wish we could have gotten to go on the same mission, so we could be together."

"I'm so sorry you were separated, Caro," Gressen said.

Sabin felt Caro pulled tighter against his brother and made sure he didn't impede her movement. How could a government separate family like that? In their world, family was the most important aspect of their lives.

"I'm sure he is doing great things on this planet Alpha you say he was sent to. What is his name?" Sabin asked.

"Scott. His name is Scott." She looked away, seeming to study the buildings as they continued to stroll toward the commons area.

"We're almost there," Gressen told them. "Everyone will be curious about you, but since there are others in the city of your Earth, they will not be as excited as they might have been."

"No one will hurt you," Veran added. "To harm a female in any way is punishable by death. You are so precious to us, that just being in the city has lifted everyone's spirit."

Sabin felt Caro draw herself up even as the tenseness he'd felt in her gait and the air surrounding her seemed to drain away. It pleased him that she wasn't afraid. He would never want her to feel frightened of anything, especially not his people. Even if she didn't welcome him as a mate, he prayed she would still be comfortable and happy in their city.

* * * *

Everywhere she looked, Caro saw beauty and pride in the city they were now a part of. The streets were clean and maintained. The family units were all clean and brightly colored. No trash or unpleasant odors marred the pleasant atmosphere. She still couldn't imagine that it was always this way. Surely, it had been spiffed up to give them a good opinion of their home. How was it possible that everything seemed so perfect? Nothing was perfect. There was always a hidden secret, a flaw. If something seemed too perfect to be true, it usually was. In her case, it always was.

As they turned a corner, what had to be the commons appeared in front of them. It reminded her of an open marketplace in Delhi, or maybe Paris, but without as many stalls of goods for sale. Instead, there were eating units all over the large open area with what she could only describe as structured tents situated throughout the area.

Directly in front of them, a large colorful stage stood about five feet off the ground with sturdy steps leading up to it. One thing she had noticed of the city was how difficult steps and stairs, as well as beds, counters, and such, would be for most of the humans who were now living among the Levassians. Their units and city had been built with towering giants in mind, not five-foot, and six-foot humans. Those steps leading up to the stage were steep in depth and far apart.

"Let's look around at the various displays, then choose what we want to eat and where to sit," Veran suggested. "I know Della has been having a fit to look around."

"You should have taken her before now," Gressen gently chided.

"Yes, you are correct, but she wanted Caro to attend with her, and I've been busy working on an empty family unit in disrepair to house some of the humans who are not comfortable where they are." Veran's skin seemed to darken slightly, as if he was embarrassed.

"That is so kind of you to help them," Caro said. "I'm sure living with strangers who look so different is uncomfortable for some of our people."

"I hope you do not feel that way, Caro." Sabin's strained voice, that was normally so calm, reminded her that she'd been so stiff around the two Levassians.

"Oh, no. I don't. I'm very comfortable where I am with you and your brother. I know I don't seem that way, but my previous life was much different from this. I'm still adjusting is all."

Now she felt embarrassed at her treatment of the two men who'd been nothing but compassionate and accommodating toward her. She had to stop comparing them to the men of Earth. They were nothing like them.

"I'm pleased that you are," Gressen said. "Come, let's look around."

Although Caro was used to being stared at—she was the center of attention due to her modeling days and her height back on Earth—Della obviously wasn't. Her friend seemed to be having trouble for the first time since she'd known the woman. In everything else, Della was one of the few women from their ship who'd bounced back in every situation. This, however, had her disquieted and agitated.

"Della, let's look over at that display. I like those colors." Caro stepped over to take her friend's hand. "We'll be right over there." Caro pointed at the tent filled with colorful materials.

"Of course," Veran said. "Kane? Could you escort them?"

At least Veran seemed to understand his mate's unease and had her other mate, a fellow human, go with them.

"Right, send me off to shop with the women. If you only knew how much the males of our race hated to shop, you'd laugh," Kane said with a good-natured grin.

Veran laughed. "I believe Della has mentioned that to me. Thus, the reason I'm sending you."

But Caro and Kane understood the real reason. She hoped Veran would enlighten her males. Caro stopped in mid-stride at the realization of what she'd just thought.

Her males. Did I just claim them? I even thought of them as males and not men. Maybe I'm becoming more adjusted than I thought, but to think of them as mine is a little premature. They might not really want me—the real me.

"Is everything okay?" Kane asked, instantly moving closer to both of them.

"Yes. Sorry. Something hit me as familiar and it stopped me for a moment. That's all. I'm fine. Let's go look before more Levassians fill the area."

Della squeezed her hand and smiled up at her. She mouthed a silent "thank you" before turning her attention to the amazing materials in front of them. They looked and touched the fine cloths, amazed at the softness and wondering how much it cost, and if they could figure out a way to barter for some.

"I'm not even sure what to do with them," Della said with a laugh. "They're so pretty though. I wonder if it ever gets windy here. They'd make great scarves, or a wonderful wrap to go over our clothes on cool days."

"I would love to have one to sleep in," Caro told her. "The texture makes me think of being held and petted."

Della chuckled. "I think you could get that feeling from Sabin and Gressen without the cloth."

Caro could feel her skin burn from her neck to her cheeks. The only consolation to her natural tan was that it didn't show blushing nearly as easily as Della's fair complexion did. Still, as hot as her cheeks felt, she was sure it was obvious.

"I'm not sure they are interested in me that way," she told her friend in a soft voice.

"Are you crazy? They're so smitten with you that they haven't taken their eyes off of you since we left their unit." Della squeezed her hand. "If you're interested in them, let them know. If not, you should ask to move to another unit. I sure don't want you to move out. I love having you so near me, but I would hate for them to get their hopes up, only to have you more interested in someone else."

"I'm not. Interested in someone else, that is. I'm just not sure if they are interested in me for me, or just that I'm a female who could give them children, young. I mean, that's all I was good for in order to be forced on this trip. And the only thing men on Earth wanted from me was my money, my contacts in the industry, or me as arm candy to show off. No one ever valued me as a person. Just what I could do for them." Caro couldn't believe she'd just bared her soul to Della, a woman she'd only known for about two months. And in an open, public place with strangers surrounding her.

"Oh, Caro. I can't imagine how you could stand the way people treated you back then. If I'd known you, I would have knocked them away from you and taken you to my favorite deli, or the zoo, or something. I loved those places and I think you would have, too. But here, I don't think you have to worry. It's not just because you are female or able to give them young. It's your personality that draws them to you. You have no idea how Sabin's face changes to pure bliss when you laugh at something. When you laugh for Gressen, his eyes sparkle like gems."

"Really? You're not just saying that to make me feel better?" Caro asked, narrowing her eyes.

"Honestly." Della sobered and lifted one hand. "On my honor, you have nothing to worry about with them."

"If you two are plotting something over there, stop it. I'm not about to let you get me into trouble." Kane's amused voice broke into their girl talk that had been mere whispers.

"Sweetheart, this has nothing to do with you." Della batted her eyelashes at the tall American Indian whose skin was the closest color to her own of all the humans from the ship. "Remember, some things don't revolve around you."

Kane's rumbling laugh turned the heads of Levassians who weren't already looking in their direction. Caro resisted the urge to slump her shoulders and duck her head.

"So, excuse me, sir." Della waved and smiled at the tall, copper-toned male watching over the merchandise.

The male seemed to panic at first, glancing in Kane's direction before slowly walking toward them. He kept a good four feet between them before he acknowledged them.

"Yes, females. What can I help you with?" He bowed his head and rested his clasped hands in front of him.

"My name is Della, and this is my friend, Caro. What is your name?" she asked him.

His eyes jerked upward, landing on Kane before moving back to stare at Della. If Caro hadn't known better, she'd have thought the male to be worried that Kane would strike him dead. Why would he think that?

"I am called Livitius, fair female. Do you wish something of me?"

Caro was sure he was trembling. She looked around to see if anyone behind them was the cause of it, but saw nothing out of the ordinary. Though the crowd of Levassians watched them with open curiosity, none of them seemed to be casting angry looks in Livitius' way.

"Why are you so nervous of us, Livitius? We aren't dangerous. We would never wish you harm," Caro said, hoping to reassure him.

"But to anger, or insult, a female would be my death. I am afraid I might say something or do something offensive to you and not know it," he confessed. "Many of us who haven't been around your people are afraid of you. None of us know enough about you to be sure we do not misspeak, or cause you distress. Already one of my friends is awaiting his execution for upsetting one of your females. I don't wish to join him."

At Caro's gasp, the poor male cringed and quickly backed away, falling to his knees. A collected gasp behind her told her that she might have just caused the death of the poor Levassian without meaning to.

Chapter Three

Before anyone could stop her, Caro hurried over to the male and bent over to rest her hands on his shoulders. She would not allow anyone to hurt him for being afraid to address her. What was wrong with these people? She'd originally thought them to be so much more civilized than humans, but maybe she'd been mistaken.

"Don't hurt him! He's afraid of us. He hasn't done or said anything wrong. I was just so overwhelmed by how beautiful and colorful the materials were. Please," Caro pleaded with Gressen and Sabin with her eyes. Surely, they would understand.

"Come here, Caro," Gressen said in a soft voice. "It's okay. You've no reason to worry."

"Then no one will hurt him?" she asked.

At Gressen's hesitation, Caro lifted her chin. "Then I won't move. He is afraid because one of his friends is now being condemned to death for no reason. I thought your people where peaceful and less blood thirsty than ours, but I was wrong. That you would execute one of your own people for something as innocent as a misunderstanding or wrong word is ludicrous."

"What? They're going to execute him?" Della glared up at Veran and stomped over to stand next to Caro before Veran could stop her.

When he took a step toward her, Vella held up one hand and lifted her chin. Evidently, Veran knew what that meant. If the situation hadn't been so serious, Caro would have laughed. Instead, she lifted her chin as well and addressed her men.

Again, I'm thinking of them as my men. Well, if they don't make this right, none of them will be my men.

"I want to speak to the rulers, council members, or whoever makes the decisions around here. This is going to stop, or I will rally all the human females I can and demand our own family unit without males. Do you understand?" Caro made sure they saw just how serious she was.

"That includes me, Veran. I thought we'd made some headway with your council, but I'm beginning to wonder if they've been completely honest with me about these changes they say they will make." Della crossed her arms.

Sabin's face had drained of as much color as he could lose while his brother's face had turned much darker. No doubt, they would regret having opened their doors to her. She was probably embarrassing them to no end, but no one was going to lose their life because of her. Other than her ability to have children, Caro didn't think she was worth the life of another, no matter what race they came from.

"Veran, go inform the council of what is happening here in the commons. See if they would hold an audience for Caro," Gressen said in a soft voice.

"Of course, sir." Veran had instantly returned to his duties with Gressen's order.

Caro wondered how that made Della's mate feel. Did he care, or did it bother him that in an instant, he went from a friend to a subordinate? It was one of the things she'd hated about society. You never really knew if your friends really where friends, or if they only treated you like that when it suited them.

The poor Levassian kneeling on the ground in front of her nearly vibrated his robes off with how much he shook in fear. Caro tried to comfort him, but just the fact that she talked to him seemed to make it worse. If this poor male lost his life because of her, she'd never be able to live with it.

"They come, Gressen." Veran had returned and slowly walked to stand next to Kane.

Caro looked at Gressen for the first time and was surprised to see a small smile on his face. Did he think this was funny? How could he be so callous? A man's life was at stake. Then she saw that he was staring at her, and before she turned away, he winked at her. It finally dawned on her that he didn't think everything was funny. He thought the fact that they were about to try and change a way of life for the Levassians was good, and he was proud of their stance. It gave her a little more courage.

"Are you ready for his?" Della whispered in her ear. "They are very uppity, stiff assholes, but they really do just want the best for their people."

Caro cleared her throat as six, extremely tall males in dark purple robes filed into the commons with several much shorter males in bright golden robes walking next to them. They moved as if they didn't walk, but glided toward them. It was almost frightening how they seemed to float inches off the ground.

"I—I'm not sure, but I don't have much of a choice now, do I," she pointed out.

"There's always a choice, Caro. You could have remained quiet and let their laws go forward, but you didn't." Della bumped her shoulder before the dignitaries floated into the immediate area.

"Gressen? What is the issue here?" one of the males asked in a seriously deep voice.

"The male kneeling in front of the female from my family unit said something that astonished her. She stepped back and the male took it to mean that he'd offended her in some way. When more males stepped toward them, intending to remove the male who'd spoken, Caro refused to allow them to take him. Then my family unit female's friend joined her." Gressen spoke confidently and clearly, though Caro knew he'd altered the truth somewhat. Why?

"Female, Caro. What is it you wish for us to do?" the male asked.

"I wish for you to change your rules concerning a male upsetting a female. We are easily upset and become emotional at the drop of a hat. You don't condemn someone to death for that alone. I wish him unharmed, and his friend who is awaiting his death released as well," she demanded.

The entire group of purple and gold robed males gasped, then erupted into arguments that she couldn't follow. She was just about to use the one thing that wasn't lady-like about her and whistle a shrill blow that her brother had taught her when the appointed leader held up his hand and roared for everyone to be silent. A hush fell over the entire commons area. Caro was sure she could have heard a butterfly flap its wings if there had been one on the planet.

"It is forbidden for a male to harm a female. There will be no change in that law," he said.

"Fine. I don't want that to change. Males shouldn't use their strength against a female. But, upsetting one is not harming them. There are too many chances that, until we become better acquainted with each other, misunderstandings and improperly used words and phrases will happen. You can't just kill a male for making a mistake that isn't harming anyone." Caro stared at the male, making sure he could see just how serious she was.

"If a female becomes upset and is with young, she could lose that child. It is forbidden to upset a female," he reiterated with force.

Soft murmurs began to fill the area in front of her. Caro drew in a deep breath and tried again.

"I'm so sorry that your females were so weak that they weren't able to handle inappropriate comments. Earth females can work in the fields without miscarrying. We can do housework, hold jobs, and never have a problem. We are a sturdy bred and able to work, have children, um, young, keep a house, and take care of our males without a problem." She looked all around her to include the entire commons area.

"We might not like doing all of that, but if it is necessary, we can, and often do, just that. When our world was young, we even fought beside our males to protect our homes and our children. We don't stand behind our males. We stand beside them. Yes, we enjoy being pampered and coddled. Females like to be told we are special and pretty, but not to the extent that it makes us weak and unable to take care of ourselves and our families. When that happens, we cease to have self-worth, and are only good for one thing, breeding. We are not cattle. We are females, and as one, I will not stand by while you murder an innocent member of your own race."

Caro put every ounce of built-up anger and pain into her glare at the gathered men in front of her. There was no way they would take this male and condemn him without harming her in the process. Then where would they be? Would they place themselves under the same rules?

To her surprise, Della added her own speech.

"I told you that this would happen if you continued to try and dictate our lives. You didn't see it as doing that. You claim you are protecting us and assuring our comfort and happiness. Where is that happiness right now? She and I both would not be able to sleep at night, much less live with ourselves with the blood of that male on our heads. We will gather all of our females and create our own family unit, and refuse your males as barbarians who only wish to subjugate us and turn us into mere breeders of your young. We will not allow it. If you should try to force us, then you are violating your own laws and should sentence yourselves to death as well. Which of you will be the first to put your head on the chopping block by laying hands on one of us?"

That got another gasp from the crowd. Everyone standing close to them took a fairly substantial step back. Caro had to roll her lips inward and bite them to keep from laughing at the sight. Were they all so afraid of their council and what would be done to them if a female cried foul? What was to stop one from getting angry for something innocent and demanding they were punished. As much as Caro wished that would never happen, there were females who would do it.

No, the law had to be changed or there would be no peace for her. She felt that many of her fellow women would be just as sickened by the law as she was.

“Why is it that the other male’s life wasn’t important enough for the female he insulted to ask that he be spared?” one of the other male members of the council asked.

“She might not realize what is at stake. This is so ludicrous that we would never have dreamed, in a million years, that a male would be executed over something so trivial. Even if she did know what the male’s fate was, she might not be allowed by the males that she is staying with to voice her objections.”

“What he said to her wasn’t that trivial,” another member in a purple robe said.

“What was it he said then?” Della asked.

The males looked at each other before one of them finally spoke. “I mean no harm or disrespect to either of you, but merely repeat his offense.”

Caro couldn’t stop the chuckle that escaped from her. “Okay, you’ve made your point and warned me. Now what did he say?”

The male cleared his throat before speaking. “He told her that her colorless skin reminded him of our moon’s glow.”

Caro gave the male one long, slow blink. That was it? That was poetry, not an insult. What was their issue?

“Are you kidding me?” Della beat her to the punch. “That’s considered a compliment. A very poetic one at that. I can’t imagine one of our females ever being insulted by that.”

The speaker turned to look at Caro. “Do you agree? This wasn’t an insult?”

“I completely agree. That was sweet and beautiful. What did the female say about it that caused the male to be condemned like that?” Caro asked.

“She covered her mouth and started crying. She didn’t say anything at all. The males of the family unit where she was staying hurried her away from the male that had upset her so," the male speaker said.

"More than likely she was crying tears of joy that someone thought so highly of her. You'd be surprised how many females of our world have never been treated as sweetly and as carefully as we've been treated here"—she waited a second—"until now, that is."

The council members turned and whispered to each other for a few seconds before parting and the original male stepped forward a step. "We are having the female and her males brought here to clear this up. I do not understand your human ways at all."

After about ten minutes, several of the golden robed males returned with three other males and a young woman who Caro hadn't remembered seeing before. She couldn't have been more than twenty-one or so. Though, she had pretty green eyes and a head full of curly red hair. Her nose was a little large and her lips a little thin. As a model, Caro knew most human men wouldn't have looked twice at her, despite how pretty her eyes and hair were. She was sure what she'd suggested had been correct now.

"Council," one of the males said and bowed. "We are here as requested. What would you wish of us?"

"The female residing in your family unit, Deon, what is her name?" the councilman Caro had deemed the leader asked.

"It is Heidi, sir." The male looked a little uneasy now, and stepped slightly away from her.

"Heidi, nothing is wrong, but we wanted to ask you some questions that your fellow females, Caro and Della, have brought to our minds. Is this okay with you?" the leader asked.

The young woman nodded, then cleared her throat after looking at the only male still standing close to her. "That is fine."

"Good. Do you remember the day a male of my race spoke to you and you started crying?"

Heidi blushed so brightly red that Caro knew she'd been right. "Yes, sir. I remember."

"Were you upset by what he said to you? Did you feel that he'd insulted you?" the leader asked.

Heidi's eyebrows lifted so high and so fast that Caro wondered if they would develop wings and fly off her face. "No! Not at all. I was so overwhelmed at how sweet what he'd said to me had been, that I broke into tears. Then Deon, Wellar, and Keigler hurried me away from him and back home, so I didn't get to tell him thank you." She looked at the various councilmen. "Did I do something wrong? I honestly meant to thank him for saying those things to me. No one ever says nice things to me like that."

Soft murmurs rose up around them once again. Caro was sure that the council would understand now. Poor Heidi. She'd been complimented, and as a result, she'd been removed from the male's presence, and the poor male has been condemned to death over tears of joy.

"Do you see what I mean? I bet if you ask Heidi, she'd like to meet him again, and maybe move to his family unit," Caro suggested.

The council gasped, then quickly quieted. Once again, the leader looked to the young woman.

"Is that true, female Heidi? Would you like to see this male again?"

Heidi looked uneasily at the three males once again standing near her. It was obvious that she didn't want to insult them. "I—I'd like that. Deon, Wellar, and Keigler are so nice to me and have been nothing but gentlemen, but perhaps I'm not really suited for them."

Silence hung heavily over the commons while the council just stared at one another for a long time. Finally, the leader of the purple robes spoke again. His voice seemed much less imposing and didn't boom as loudly as before.

"We shall meet with the rise of our suns and discuss how to amend this law so that innocent males are not harmed for these misunderstandings, as you call them. Until then, this male has done nothing to harm these females and is without blame. This other male that female Heidi wishes to see again will be released, and the blight over his head erased. No fault is placed on him."

Caro breathed a sigh of relief and hugged Della. The male still on his knees in front of her didn't move, though he was no longer vibrating like the Eveready Bunny anymore. She walked around to look down at him. Holding out her hand, she waited for him to see it.

"Please get up. I'm sorry, but I don't remember your name. I'm so sorry this happened to you. Will you ever forgive me?" she asked. Those close enough to hear gasped at her words.

The male didn't take her hand, but did rise. He finally looked down at her with a tentative smile. "I'm called Livitius. I do not cast blame on one as gracious as you. I'm overwhelmed at your bravery, and the pity you took on one such as me. I am forever in your debt and would willing serve you should you have need." He quickly looked over at Della. "I am equally in your debt as well, female."

Della laughed. "Livitius, you are an amazing male, but I have two slaves who are willing to take good care of me. I hope you find a female to give you all of the love you deserve."

Caro watched as Kane strode over to pick Della up and throw her over his shoulder. To the astonishment of everyone who could see or hear, he landed a hefty swat to her ass. Veran only chuckled at her growl. Everyone waited to see what she'd do. Caro had no doubt her friend would surprise them yet again. And she did.

"Do it again, slave. Do it again!"

Chapter Four

"That was very compassionate, but also very brave," Sabin told the surprising female as they walked home after taking a brief meal.

"I, too, believe it was most gracious," Gressen said.

Sabin watched the brief play of emotions cross her face before she hid them. He realized she was very good at closing down her expressions. Why? He'd yet to see any of the other females do such a thing. Why was she so different? He knew that part of that difference was what had attracted him to her in the first place. While he didn't want to change her unique personality, he did want to know why she seemed so reserved at times.

"You're not upset with me over it?" she asked, stopping and looking from one to the other of them.

"Not at all, Caro. I believe, between you and your friend, the female Della, some of the old laws and rules that are of no use to us will be changed. They were put into place many, many years ago to try to protect and save our dying race and the precious females who were left to us," Sabin told her.

"These laws no longer help us, but hurt us," Gressen added. "With our races so different, there will be many mistakes made in what we say and how we say it. I applaud your intelligence in figuring out what had actually happened."

"The other females have thought more about their own comfort and fears than how they were affecting our males. I do not fault them at all, but finding a female as thoughtful and unselfish as you is a true treasure. Thank you for your courage, sweet Caro." Sabin gently touched the side of her face with the palm of his hand. To his surprise, she rubbed her face against his skin for a brief second before stepping away.

"Let us return to our unit. I'm sure you are most exhausted. Della will worry if you do not return soon." Gressen smiled across Caro's head at him and gave a quick nod.

To his amazement, Caro reached out to both of them for their hands, and smiled as they continued walking along the smooth road. Sabin felt hope for the first time that he could remember. Not so much that their sweet Caro would turn to them to be part of their family unit, but that there would once again be children amongst them, and happy males who would joy in them, despite not having them as their own. There would be hope, once again, for the continuation of their race.

Sabin paid special attention to his grip to make sure he didn't let his enthusiasm transfer to his much stronger hand and crush Caro's soft, delicate one. Causing her distress for any reason would devastate him. Seeing her sweet smiles warmed his heart. When they were directed at either his brother or himself, Sabin could easily walk on air with happiness.

"Here we are. I wonder if the others have retired to their personal unit, or if they are in the common room?" Gressen mused aloud.

When they walked into the entrance, Sabin could hear Della's laugh and smiled. This would make Caro happy. He was sure the two females would want to discuss their escapade. Perhaps he and the other males could talk about it as well. They needed to think of other issues that could arise that would distress their females. Sabin smiled at that thought. If he and his brother were lucky, Caro would indeed be their female.

Almost as soon as they made it all the way inside and Gressen had closed the door, Della's squeal of delight followed her around the corner as she blew into the entrance and wrapped Caro in her exuberant embrace. Nothing about the female would ever be described as meek or serene. If it weren't for the air of caution in Caro, he would equate serenity with her.

"I can't believe we did that! Actually, you were the one who did it. I just joined you. You are a true hero, Caro." Della squeezed her again and Sabin had to restrain himself from extracting Caro from her arms, for fear of bruising her delicate skin.

"I can't quite believe it myself, but to know that, because of me, a man was executed? I couldn't live with myself knowing that. It's barbaric," she said with a shiver.

"Come on. We need to talk about discussing these things with the other females. I don't want any of them to cause something like that to happen by accident," Della said.

"I'm a little worried that some of them will start trouble just because they can. There are a couple of them who I am not fond of, Della. If we tell them what they could cause to happen, they just might try it out to see what sort of power they have over the men here."

Sabin stilled at that statement as the two females disappeared around the corner. He never would have equated cruelness with a female. From what Caro said, these women had the duplicity to cause problems in order to gain power. What sort of power would they wish to have that a male wouldn't bestow on them anyway?

It hit him as he thought more about what Caro and Della had said. The other males talked around him as they retired to his and Gressen's smaller common area. Those women might wish the power to cause males to ply them with treasures in order to win their favor. It would give the females some manner of control over them so that they might lose control of their emotions and civility, and actually fight over them. That thought worried him greatly.

"What do you think, brother?" Gressen asked.

"I'm sorry. I had my thoughts elsewhere. What did you say?" Sabin asked.

"I believe it would be in our best interest to hold a discussion with the council on the areas we feel are prone to cause problems with these new and different females. Kane has several things he believes might become future issues for us," Gressen patiently repeated to him.

"Yes. I believe you are right. Caro and Della's comments have caused me to think that we must learn more about the females of the human race. I believe Kane will be most informative, and should be present with these conversations," Sabin said.

"I'm not sure I'm the best person to help in this. I'm different in some ways from the other males of our world. One of them may be more suited to helping with the council," Kane said.

"To be forthright, Kane, I have no trust for the other males at this point. They withheld information that could have been very important. While I understood the need for this at first, once they realized we meant you no harm, they should have enlightened us out of good faith." Gressen shook his head. "No, you are a most straightforward and honorable male."

Verán nodded. "Then it is settled. The council is meeting at the rising of our two suns. We need to settle for the night to be fresh and clear minded to join them."

They all stood up, and Sabin had to smile when Kane stretched and yawned. Veran, Kane's partner with Della, smiled and shook his head. Sabin realized that since spending time with the human male, Veran had become more like him. The male smiled more and seemed more relaxed than he'd seen a male of their race before. It was good. Maybe with the addition of the human females, more of their men would become freer with their emotions. Of course, with less restraint and more freedom of their emotions, they would be prone to all emotions, including anger. That wouldn't strengthen their race at all. They needed to think deeply on these things.

* * * *

Caro yawned as she opened her eyes. The thick curtains kept almost all of the bright light from Levasso's dual suns from streaming into the room. She knew that to step outside between their noon and their sixteenth hour would make them extremely tired, hot, and thirsty. It would also burn their eyes if they didn't wear protective eyewear. The males of the planet were used to it and many didn't need to use them.

She had a lot to learn about their world, but knowing the dark, orange suns could burn your eyes and that the rich, blue lichen grew like grass across the ground and up nearly three feet of the gray tree trunks wasn't what she or any of the other women needed know. They needed to understand the males and their past. They needed to learn more about the females they had loved before they died.

While Caro could appreciate how clean everything felt, even the air she breathed, she also knew that there were dangers she still didn't know about—like finding out that dehydration for humans could happen in a matter of an hour if they didn't constantly drink while outside.

She would need to depend on Gressen and Sabin to protect her from the things she didn't know were dangerous because she needed to concentrate on how to keep the females from causing even more havoc among the males of Levasso. Without knowing what could trigger another misunderstanding, Caro worried that what had happened already could happen again. She needed to talk to the others and caution them.

It took a great deal of effort to roll out of bed that morning. She'd lain awake a long time into the night thinking about what she'd learned of the males, and how their women could affect them and their way of life. Della thought the changes would be for the better, and that the males of Levastah, the only real city left on the planet, would welcome additional freedoms. Caro wasn't so sure about that. Too many of the women from the ship were headstrong. Unlike the submissive Heidi, who was just thankful that someone had paid her a complement, many of the women were used to such treatment, and would see the opportunity to make the most of it.

After cleaning up and dressing in one of the beautiful robe-like dresses that had been made for her, Caro left her room and walked toward the eating area. It was difficult to call it a kitchen since you couldn't tell anything about it until something was accessed. It all disappeared into the walls, much like the lavatory and shower enclosure in her room. Nifty for small places, but unsettling just the same.

"Caro. You look amazing this morn. Did you sleep well? After the evening at the commons, we were worried you would be too distraught to settle." Gressen crossed the room to touch her cheek and look into her eyes. "Sabin, perhaps you should take a look at her. I hope you're not growing ill, Caro. You're eyes are puffy and it's dark beneath them. Do you feel well?"

Caro knew she looked less than her usual well put together self, but didn't think anyone would notice. She had no makeup to cover the effects of her long night. Normally, she would have covered the effects of a sleepless night with concealer.

"I'm fine, Gressen. I'm not ill. I just didn't sleep well so I have circles beneath my eyes is all. We get those if we don't get the right amount of sleep." Caro made sure her smile showed none of the anxiety that had built up over the enormous effect of their crashing on the planet. They could easily make changes that would ruin the Levassian culture and social norms. She didn't want that.

"I will check her over anyway, brother. It doesn't hurt to be cautious since they are not from our atmosphere. Then, there is the issue of our two suns. I'm sure that drains them," Sabin said.

"If you didn't get enough sleep, Caro, once Sabin is sure nothing more is wrong, you will go back to bed and continue your sleep cycle." Gressen smiled down at her before walking over to press his hand against what she knew would be the equivalent to their refrigerators.

"I'm not going back to bed, Gressen. I'm fine. Sometimes my mind races and it takes me more time to fall asleep than normal. Having an occasional sleepless night doesn't harm me." Caro avoided Sabin when he brought over one of the diagnostic thingies he used.

Instead, she walked to where Gressen worked with something that looked like butter. Oblivious to her intentions, the poor male jumped when she grabbed him by the upper arm and pulled him around to face her. To say surprise washed over his face would be an understatement. He looked completely shocked and uncomfortable. It made Caro stop and drop her hands. Had she unwittingly done something so improper that it would ruin their relationship?

"I—I'm sorry. I didn't mean to scare you. I just wanted you to look at me instead of ignoring me when I was talking to you," she said, even as she fought to keep from crying.

What was wrong with her? Tears where not something she indulged in, even when they would have been expected. They showed weakness, and in her line of work, one couldn't show one ounce of weakness or they'd have eaten her like a tasty snack.

"Oh, Caro, sweet Caro. You did nothing wrong. I am just not used to a female touching me. It has been many, many cycles, or, as you say, years ago. I welcome your touch anytime you would wish to touch me." He smiled down at her and started to touch her chin, but noticed the buttery looking substance on his hand and frowned.

Caro hid a smile at the expression that changed the noble lines of his face into one of disgust. It was as if he was angry with his fingers for being dirty so that he couldn't touch her. That thought made her smile, despite her efforts to hide it.

"What did you wish for me to look at you for?" he asked as he quickly cleaned his hands.

"I just want to make sure you understand that I'm fine and don't need to go back to bed. Gressen, I'm not a child to be told what to do as if I have no say in it."

Sabin walked around to stand next to his brother and cocked his head as if trying to understand what she was saying. There were times that she thought the males of the planet looked a lot like a wild animal when they did that.

"I would like to scan your front now, Caro. The readings I am getting from behind are inconclusive." Sabin held up the tablet-looking thing and smiled at her.

Caro rolled her eyes and gave up. "Fine, get it over with."

Sabin's smile faded slightly, but he moved the tablet back and forth then up and down her body. While he looked at whatever data he could see on the instrument, Caro resumed her explanation of human ways related to sleep and rest.

"Humans need anywhere from six to ten hours of sleep, on average, a night. Some operate better on less sleep than others. Some need nine and ten hours, at least three times a week, to function normally. Everyone has the occasional sleepless or restless night. It's normal for us. I don't need to go back to bed. If I need more sleep, I can always take a nap." Caro stopped there and tried to analyze how her speech had gone over with Gressen and Sabin.

"She is essentially fine, brother, but her stress level is elevated," Sabin said.

"Well, I'm not surprised. She is distressed with our wanting her to be well rested. I'm not sure how to address this issue," Gressen said to his brother.

"Talking about me like I'm not even here sure as heck isn't going to help the issue!" Caro stuck her hands on her hips and glared at the two men. "What is so hard about including me in this conversation when it's about me in the first place?"

Gressen cocked his head in that "I'm not sure how to deal with you" stance and smiled. "We only want what is best for your health and happiness, Caro. I fail to see how allowing you to continue, while still requiring sleep, is doing that."

"That's just it. You don't allow me to do anything! It's my decision what I do and don't do. Not yours, Sabin's, or the council's. I'm a sentient being who has freedom of choice and the ability to think for myself. Either treat me like that, or I need to move somewhere else. Surely there's an empty home or pod, or whatever, where I can live." Caro had barely finished her angry tirade before Gressen picked her up in his arms and carried her out of the kitchen area with Sabin following close behind.

Caro was so startled by the very abnormal behavior that she couldn't utter a word, and knew her mouth was hanging open in a very un-ladylike way. Sabin's face as she looked over Gressen's shoulder showed no clue to what he was thinking. That bothered her since Sabin, more often than Gressen, allowed expressive hints to what he was thinking to show on his face. Not this time, though.

"Gressen? What are you doing? What's going on?" she finally managed to get out just as he slammed his hand on the pad next to his door. "Gressen? Sabin?"

Neither male answered her. Instead, Gressen laid her on his bed, close to the middle. To her surprise, Sabin then removed her shoes.

Oh, so that's it. They're going to make me take a nap for my own good. I'm not letting them treat me like a child. I know when I need to rest and when I'm good enough to catch up on sleep later.

Just as Caro was about to say as much, Gressen pulled his tunic off and sat on the edge of the bed before removing his foot coverings. A dip in the other side of the bed had her whipping her head around to find Sabin doing the same thing.

Oh, God. What have I done? Surely they aren't going to try and force sex on me. Are they?

Caro prepared to fight them if necessary. She'd never have believed it of them. They were both so calm and sweet to her, seeing to her every need almost to the point of driving her insane with it. How had she so incompetently misjudged them? Usually her assessment of the people around her was dead on. Maybe that was where she'd made the mistake though. These weren't human men. They were a different race. They were Levassians, and had different ideals and beliefs.

"W—what's going on, guys? What are you doing?" Caro finally asked.

She scooted closer to the opposite side from Gressen, but Sabin was already lying on the bed with his face turned her way.

"We are going to rest with you, Caro. I don't know any other way to convince you to take better care of yourself." Gressen relaxed on the bed and turned to look at her. "If it were not for the great differences between our planet's atmosphere and yours, we would not be as concerned, but there is. In addition, there is the fact that we have two suns that produce more light and heat than you're accustomed to. Rest, Caro. We will rest with you."

She had no words. Suddenly she was exhausted. Between the lack of sleep, and bouncing from one extreme with her emotions to the other, Caro knew they were right and that she was making too much of a simple subject. What was the subject again?

Chapter Five

Sabin slowly returned to consciousness with the feel of his arms around something warm and soft. The scent of something inviting filled his head with sexual thoughts he hadn't had since he'd been a young male. His male flesh hardened as he shifted, alerting him to the fact that someone was in the bed with him, and he had his arms around them. In a flash, his eyes opened wide in panic.

How did I end up in bed with my brother? Why would I ever embrace him like this? Am I developing a brain infection? I need to allow one of the other healers to scan me for disease.

He started to remove his arms when it finally occurred to him that his brother was in no means soft to the touch, nor did he smell of heaven. The morning's discussion with Caro returned to him and Sabin relaxed with a relieved sigh. He wasn't sick after all.

Caro shifted in her sleep, rubbing her extremely sexy ass against his already engorged member.

Wait. What was it Veran had been teaching them? Females have cocks and men have pussies. I need to remember those words to talk to sweet Caro in her own language.

The way her ass caressed his pussy had him aching all over. He couldn't stop himself from thrusting against her when she moved again.

A soft "mmmm" made him smile. She seemed to like his pussy against her cock. Could they convince her to share with them, become their female? To have a mate would be a wonderful thing indeed. If she agreed to bear them young, they would be doubly blessed.

He carefully caressed her shoulder through the robes that had been made for her. They hid some of her body, but left enough to tantalize the male's senses. They didn't expect a female to completely cover herself, but he and his brother had both been relieved when she'd taken to the feminine robes over the pantaloons-type outfit that Della normally wore.

They'd made sure only the finest of soft cloths were used for Caro's clothes. Nothing coarse or prickly for their wonderful female. She deserved the very best they could obtain for her.

She turned in her sleep to wrap her arms around him. Her head lay nestled against his chest and the heat of her exhaled breath tickled his chest. Where his brother was smooth chested, he had a small area of hair. When she rubbed her cheek against it, his pussy swelled to the point of pain, and he groaned aloud.

"Brother. What is she doing to you?" Gressen's deep voice whispered so softly he almost didn't hear it.

"I don't know, brother. Just holding her and feeling her soft body has me aching to release inside of her. What am I to do? If I move, I might wake her," he whispered back.

"Don't move. We will remain like this until she wakes on her own." Gressen gently laid his arm over her waist and snuggled against her back as Sabin had done earlier.

"She smells like warm sunshine after a long rain," Gressen said.

"I know. I love how she feels so right between us. I want nothing more than to remain here until my end. Is that normal?" Sabin didn't think it was.

"It is. Males who had females, or remember them better than we do, talked of this. The few we've been around and bred with were not like our females, and we felt no affection toward them. Caro is very different."

"She is. Her name shouldn't even be spoken in the same thought as those females. She is more than joining. She is forever."

Gressen nodded across from him with their sweet Caro lying slumbering between them. Her soft skin and warm, tan complexion made him want to run his hands and mouth all over her to find the places on her body that would please her.

His brother's strangled moan, along with the way his head lay back and his eyes were tightly closed, told him that Caro was rubbing her ass against his pussy now. He knew just how good and, at the same time, how painful it could be.

Again, Caro moaned. Neither of them could stop the instant need to touch and caress her amazing body. Gressen moved his hand lightly up and down her arms, then eased farther around to gently touch her cloth-covered breasts, rubbing lightly over the already distended nipples.

Sabin could tell from the way her body arched out to press more of her breasts into his brother's hands that Caro liked it. He wanted to touch her as well and know that he was bringing her pleasure. He lowered one hand to where her robes had slipped up her thighs, and touched her bare skin. Instantly, warmth and silky skin became an addiction he had no remorse over. The only thing better than running his hands across her smooth skin was if he could taste it and kiss it.

He leaned in and inhaled just below her ear in the curve of her neck. Her heady scent took away his ability to think logically, and Sabin brushed his slightly open lips across her jaw. The light taste of her went straight to his head just as her scent had. How in the name of all Levasso would he ever be able to stop with one touch—one taste—of her addicting body? Every place on her body was pure perfection in his eyes. The way her ass flared and the soft round area of her abdomen gave him dirty thoughts of what he would love to try with her.

Guilt over what he wanted soon turned to desire as she moved between him and his brother. Her head tilted and rolled toward him so that her face rested beneath his chin, on his shoulder. Before he could get over how good it felt for her to be there, something tickled his neck and Sabin realized Caro was licking him.

"What is it, brother?" Gressen's voice still sounded strained.

"She's licking my neck. Suns, I can feel it all the way down to my pussy. It's throbbing."

"Your what? Where did you hear this?" Gressen said with a much different tone to his voice now.

"Kane and Veran were trying to teach me the words they use on Earth for things we might need to know. A man's reproductive part is called a pussy, and the female's opening is called a cock. They are very odd terms, but I wanted to know what might make her feel more natural with us, should she agree to be our mates." Sabin could hear his brother making odd noises on the other side of Caro.

"Sabin, I'm so glad you haven't used them with Caro yet," he said, still sounding very different. "You have them backward, brother. Our member is called a cock or a dick. Not sure why there are two names, but a female's sexual part is called her pussy or vagina. Again, the two names are unnecessary to me."

"I don't understand. I never confuse terms like that. Surely they weren't trying to confuse me. I can't see Veran doing that. I don't know Kane well enough, but didn't get a sense of treachery about him." Sabin was very glad he'd made the mistake with his brother and not Caro.

"I am sure it's that we are both trying to learn so much so quickly to make our Caro happy and satisfied with us. I do not believe they would intentionally do such a thing."

"I think it would be a good idea for us to ask Kane to give some talks on terms and expectations the females may have, so that our males are not at a disadvantage and unknowingly make mistakes or upset the females."

"I agree. We will talk to Veran and Kane about this the next time we are in the common room together, while the females talk with each other." Gressen sighed. "She is teasing me so sweetly without even knowing it. My, um, cock is very hard and aches to fill her pussy, Sabin."

He knew just how his brother felt. His was hard and his sex organs were tight and itchy. What were they called? He was sure they didn't refer to them as sex organs.

"Gressen, did they tell you what our sex organs are called?"

His brother groaned. "Yes, they are called balls, gonads, or testis, I believe. They must think they are very important to have three different names."

"Well, at least balls sound closer to their shape than the other words that are so different. However, I've heard some of the other males make comments using the word balls in the context of someone being bold and have the nerve to go up against their leader, the Major John Lance."

Gressen didn't say anything for a short time. "I have noticed that they tend to use one word that can have more than one meaning at times. It is an odd practice. We will explore that as well when we talk to Kane. I don't like that our males could use a word in the wrong context and be ridiculed, or insult someone because of this."

"This is true." Sabin shuttered when, once again, Caro ran her open mouth across his neck, then the tip of her warm, wet tongue trailed along his shoulder before she moaned and rested her head there.

"Gressen, this is torture. If we don't leave her soon, I'm going to lose control and touch her more. I don't believe that is a good idea when she is not ours."

"Yes, brother. You are right. We will move from the bed—soon. Soon, brother."

* * * *

Caro woke to soft whispers around her. She froze, aware that both males were in the bed with her, and tried to remember why they were there. As she thought back, she remembered that they'd insisted she lay down for a little longer since she'd not slept well the night before. While it had been sweet and caring on their part, she didn't like someone else dictating what she could and couldn't do.

They hadn't really done that though, had they? In order to assure that I'm taking care of myself, they even got in bed with me so I wouldn't be alone. How can I get angry over that?

Yet she'd gotten angry earlier. Now that she'd had some rest, Caro didn't feel that way any longer. They'd been right, but she wasn't about to let them know that.

As she lay between them letting her mind wonder, Caro realized that Gressen was behind her with a very noticeable erection situated between her ass cheeks. The clothes between them did little to mask the imposing size of his cock.

As they whispered between themselves about the different names for their penises, Caro became more aware of her body and the fact that she was a little more than aroused. Not only that, but she was unconsciously rubbing her mouth along Sabin's neck. She was enjoying the way he tasted and smelled. She wanted to run her hands through his hair to see what it felt like. The tight braids had to be uncomfortable to sleep on. Did he removing them and sleep with his hair free?

Gressen didn't wear braids like his brother, and some of the other males. His bold, sweet corn colored hair complemented his golden bronze skin. Though she hadn't really touched it, she thought it looked wiry, but wasn't sure.

It took all of her strength not to moan in appreciation when she involuntarily pressed her ass back against Gressen's thick cock. When he groaned, she nearly broke out in laughter. She loved having that effect on the male. For some reason, it seemed more important and arousing than it had with the men back on Earth. With them, it seemed a given since they pretty much got hard at anyone with a hole or breasts. She didn't sense that about the Levassians.

Caro decided to see how far she could push them before they called her on her actions. She became bolder with tasting Sabin's skin along his neck and down to his shoulder. Then she traveled back the way she'd come with her tongue, licking a wet line up around his jaw and gently nibbling there.

While she'd been doing that, Caro realized she'd started rubbing her ass against Gressen's hard cock, making little circles with her ample ass. He responded with a strangled moan, and tightened his hold on her breasts. He had his hands there and Caro hadn't noticed until just then. The feel of those massive hands was like a heavy weight that made her feel safe and secure. She liked the feel of his heated flesh covering them, and wished only that he'd play with them.

She nearly begged him to do just that, but bit her lip and attempted to steady her breathing before she resumed using her mouth and tongue on Sabin. She noticed that both men moved their hands over her body a little more. Sabin gently squeezed her waist while Gressen began doing the same to her breasts. The simultaneous sensations soothed her even as they aroused her. She didn't feel used or as if she was just a handy hole to the two Levassians.

To her shock, Sabin rested his mouth against her forehead near her hairline. The in and out of his warm breath sent chills along her arms. The innocent touch held just as much sensual feeling as Gressen's hands on her breasts. Then he kissed her there and all innocence evaporated in the heat of her desire.

It hit her hard when he began reigning soft kisses all across her head and lightly across her eyes. The sweetness of it couldn't overwhelm the silky feel of his lips against her skin. She'd never felt so cherished before. It was as if she wasn't just a body to be used or displayed, but an actual person—a female who was important to them.

Even as that thought gave her pleasure and comfort, another followed fast on its heels. She was also their only hope of a child and a mate. Wouldn't any of the females from their ship have been just fine with them? Was she really all that special?

I shouldn't read too much into this. I'll only get my heart stepped on again if I do.

But they didn't realize she was awake, or they wouldn't have been whispering things to each other she was sure they didn't mean for her to know about. Why, if all she was to them was a means to having a family, would they be so tender and seem to gain joy just from touching her when she wouldn't know they were spending all this time and effort loving her?

That's what it actually felt like, too. It felt as if they were making slow, delicious, sweet love to her. If they were always like this, Caro doubted she would be able to resist them if she truly wanted to. No one had ever treated her like this before. She'd been a sex object back on Earth. Nothing more. Here, she might be a way to give the males children and a mate, but they were honest and truly seemed to care about her, which was why they were all in her bed together.

Caro made a decision that surprised her. She planned to seduce the two males and make them hers.

Chapter Six

Caro stretched slowly, nuzzling up against Sabin's shoulder and pushing back with her hips and ass against Gressen's pelvis and bulging dick. The swift intake of air by the two males resonated deep in her cunt so that she felt the slickening of her passage. In all the years she'd been sexually active, and through every relationship she'd ever had, Caro had never felt this level of arousal before.

Now she knew that it really was possible to drip with need. She'd read hundreds of romance books where the heroine dripped she was so aroused, but had never believed them.

Good Lord! I don't need any more convincing that I've been seeing the wrong men. If Sabin and Gressen do this to me without lifting a finger, I'll have their young and be a happy mate.

It felt as if every cell in her body was alive for the first time. She felt the air as it moved over her skin. Her heartbeat echoed in her ears and at every pulse point in her body. This was what sex was supposed to be like. It was supposed to awaken things inside of you that you hadn't even known was there before. It reaffirmed that life was worth living and worth taking chances. Caro had every intention of taking a chance with Sabin and Gressen.

Before she chickened out, Caro licked down Sabin's neck to his chest, and continued until she found a nipple nestled in a small patch of course hair. The little bud was much larger than a human male's was. She had much more to hold onto once she closed her lips around the flesh and sucked.

"What? Gressen! She's sucking on my chest." Sabin's surprised and slightly panicked voice almost startled her into letting go, but she managed to resist and sucked even harder on his nipple.

"Does it hurt?" Gressen asked him. "Should I try and remove her?"

"No. It feels good, but I wasn't expecting it. I didn't know females did that to us like we would want to suck on their breasts."

"Neither did I," Gressen said. "Is she awake?"

Caro smiled and released the treat from her mouth. "I'm awake. Now leave me alone while I enjoy myself. I'll get to you in a minute, Gressen."

She returned to Sabin's yummy chest and attacked the opposite nipple with as much enthusiasm as the first one. Caro loved the way he squirmed and moaned as she sucked and nipped on it. The feel of his hands touching her shoulders, then her hair with barely there pressure made her smile. The poor male was afraid to do anything that might upset her and make her stop what she was doing.

Finally, when she started licking and kissing down his chest to his abdomen, the male dug his hands into her hair and lightly massaged her scalp as if he had no control of his hands. She knew the feeling. Some lust-filled succubus had possessed her and was turning her into something wild and unfettered.

"What are you doing, Caro?" Sabin's voice sounded breathy and worried. "Gressen, what do I do?"

"Nothing, brother. Let her do as she will with you. Caro would not hurt us, would you, Caro?" Gressen asked.

"Oh, I'll make it hurt so good, Gressen. You'll beg me to do it again." Caro couldn't believe it was her voice with its sexy, husky sound.

Before either Gressen or Sabin could say anything, Caro pulled Sabin's pants down and reaching her goal. She licked a long wet line up his impressive shaft before sucking on just the cockhead. She dragged her tongue across the slit at the top, savoring the drop of pre-cum that gathered there, and hummed her pleasure at the odd taste.

Sabin's yell echoed in the room as if they were in a concert hall. The startled shout had Gressen going to his knees on the bed, positioning himself above them.

"Sabin, did she bite you?"

"Suns, no. She's sucking and licking on my cock. Gressen, it is amazing. How did we not know of this?" Sabin's words trailed off as he threw his head back when she took him as far into her mouth and down her throat as she could manage.

"I—I can't stand it. I'm going to lose my seed. Stop, Caro. Please stop," he pleaded.

Caro considered ignoring him, but didn't want to do something that might be wrong in their eyes. She could teach them her ways just as easy as they could teach her their ways. She slowly pulled off of his long, slick dick, giving the rounded head one long last lick before looking up at him.

"Did I do something wrong, Sabin? Didn't you like it?" she purred with just the right amount of lowered eyelids to add to the effect. She wanted them both under her spell for just once.

"N–no. You didn't do anything at all wrong, Caro, but I didn't want to spill my seed in your mouth. I didn't think you would like that, or I could choke you." He drew in a deep breath. "That was amazing."

"This is something that you do on Earth to your males? I know that the males lick your pussy and it is something our males have said was done to give the females release before the actual mating," Gressen said. "Would you allow us to do that for you, sweetness?"

Caro lost all thought of being a sex kitten and seducing them. Gressen had turned the tables on her with his innocent request. How could she possibly resist them? They seemed to draw pleasure by making her feel good or just seeing her smile. She wanted to embrace that so much, but fear still held a small part of her back.

"Honey, you can do that any time you want to. Believe me, females love it," she told him.

"Will you let us do that now, Caro?" Sabin asked in a hesitant voice.

"If you really want to, I'd love it. If you don't enjoy it, though, I'd rather you didn't do it. There are too many other things we can do for each other without one of us trying to please the other with something we don't really enjoy," she told them.

What had happened to her? Did she really just say that?

I'm possessed. Would I really give up oral sex if they didn't like it? Is the atmosphere doing something to my head?

Caro didn't have a clue, but for some reason the thought of them wanting so badly to please her that they would tongue her off, despite not enjoying, or worse yet, really disliking it, made her feel queasy. She really liked them too much to expect that. A part of her even thought she might love them a little. They'd gone out of their way to make her comfortable on their alien world.

"We want to try it, sweetness," Sabin told her with a smile.

"Hey, I won't stop you. Please, be my guest." She lay back on the bed, hoping they would enjoy it, but understanding if they didn't.

The two males knelt on either side of her and began untying the sash that held her robes tighter around her. Then they shoved the hem of the garment up her thighs with a reverent anticipation that gave her goosebumps all over.

"Ah, such perfect skin and strong legs," Gressen whispered.

"They have a pleasing shape and feel to them," Sabin added as he touched and squeezed her claves before running his hands up her thighs.

They slowly pushed the fabric all the way to her waist, then rolled her from one side to the other so that they could completely remove it over her head. Caro hadn't thought about being completely bare to them. She wore nothing beneath the robes since the only underwear she had was drying. They had not made underwear for the females yet, as they had never seen it before.

For a full minute, the two males stared at her as if they couldn't believe their luck. Then Gressen crawled over her leg to lay between her thighs. She wanted to watch him as he explored her for the first time, but Sabin had other plans. The much quieter male licked up the side of one breast. His tongue seemed much smoother than the men of Earth, but it was much longer. While some men like Gene Simmons of the rock band KISS was known for his tongue being extraordinarily long, the average man's was much shorter. Sabin's could actually curl around her nipple, producing a sensation she'd never felt before.

That was, until Gressen dragged his long tongue up her slit and around her clit. When both men used their tongues on her at the same time, Caro saw stars. She hadn't been prepared for anything as arousing as this. They would rule her with sex before it was over with. She was almost positive that they'd already turned her into an addict. God, what would happen when they actually had full intercourse? Would she even survive?

She vowed right then that, if she lived past this, she would talk to Della to see if this was normal, or if they were some sort of aberrations among their race. Surely this wasn't normal. No wonder Della was always smiling and let the males in her life do all sorts of crazy things to her. If they were half as good as Sabin and Gressen, she didn't see how Della ever had enough energy to get out of bed.

* * * *

Gressen was always in control. He led the elite protectors and security teams and made sure the city and those who lived on its outskirts were safe. Yet one alien female had broken down all of his defenses to rule him using his own body to do it. He wanted more than anything to please her so that she would remain with him and his brother, and grace them with her smiles and laughter. How had this happened?

No doubt Veran would understand, but the rest of his men? No, they would think him weak and not worthy to lead them anymore. He had to regain some measure of control before he became an embarrassment to his uniform. But not yet. There would be plenty of time to regain control.

But, what if I can't? I fear she has bewitched me with her beauty and grace.

The first taste of her pussy settled on his tongue, leaving a spicy flavor he'd never encountered before. He wouldn't say it was delicious, but it was an addicting taste that he was sure he'd beg to receive if she tried to refuse him. Even now, he didn't want to explore her sex because he wanted to taste more of her.

Gressen groaned when he lost control and plunged his tongue deep into her cunt. He barely registered her cry as the tangy taste of her juices filled his mouth. Nothing had ever tasted so good. Yes, he'd had many exceptional meals at the commons, but this was different. This was the essence of the female he wished to be his and Sabin's mate. It was a private part of her that no one else would ever taste again.

He barely recognized his own moan as he plunged his tongue deeper and deeper into her warm moist cavern before circling the sensitive button he'd been told they called a clit. He'd doubted Kane's promise of driving a female crazy by flicking it and sucking on it, but now he was a believer. Just blowing a breath across it now that she was aroused elicited gasps and pleading for more.

"Brother, she's begging you. Don't make her wait. Give her whatever she wishes. I can't stand to see her like this," Sabin urged.

Gressen reluctantly pulled back from the delight of her pussy to smile up at where his brother lay at the level of her generous breasts. His mouth was wet and her nipples rosy and swollen from his ministrations. If not for his brother's distress over their, hopefully, mate's mewling, Sabin would have looked pleased with his position.

"I will, Sabin. I want her to need it so badly it hurts. Then when I bring her completion, she'll enjoy it more. It is what Kane suggested to satisfy her."

Caro's head thrashed back and forth as he ran one finger up and down her slit while he reassured his brother. When he dipped his finger only a little bit into her pussy, she hissed and bucked her hips, shoving his finger deeper into her cunt. He quickly withdrew it, afraid that he would hurt her. Their fingers were large and blunt with slightly longer, claw-like nails compared to the human's.

"Careful, sweet Caro. I don't want to hurt you," he said.

"Do something, anything, Gressen. I need to come," she wailed. Then she reached up and grabbed his brother's braids, and pulled him down until their mouths touched.

He'd seen Kane and Veran kiss Della, but hadn't yet done this himself. To see Sabin with his mouth against Caro had his cock growing thicker with anticipation. Caro led the kiss, but it wasn't long before his brother took her head in both of his hands and relieved her of it.

Gressen stopped watching and returned to his treat, making sure to give equal time to her clit and her female flesh they called pussy lips. Then he'd plunge his tongue in and out of her cunt, lapping up every drop of her sweet honey before starting all over again. When she started bucking against his tongue thrusts, Gressen decided it was time. He lapped at the tiny bud at the top of her slit before sucking, then nipping it lightly with his teeth.

Caro screamed, arching her back and clawing at the covers beneath her. Sabin was thrown off of her and nearly rolled off the bed. He caught himself, and returned to her side to try and help her relax once she'd settled down some. Gressen hadn't been expecting that at all. Now he worried that he'd bitten too hard and hurt her. Fear and disgust darkened his heart at the thought.

"Caro. Please, Caro. Are you okay? Did I harm you? I promise I didn't mean to. I only wanted to give you pleasure. Tell me, Caro. Please," he pleaded.

Caro put one hand up, but only panted with her eyes closed. She shook her head but still didn't say anything. Sabin looked over at him with enough worry for both of them, but he didn't say anything.

"I—I'm fine. Give me a minute. Got to catch my breath," she told them between pants.

Gressen let out a slow breath. She sounded as if she wasn't upset, but until she told him why she'd screamed, he wouldn't feel comforted. Neither of the other males had mentioned that Della would scream while they pleasured her. With the way their living quarters were soundproofed, it would be impossible for them to ever hear if that had happened.

"I'm fine, Gressen. That was amazing. God! Your tongue is huge! It's like a snake," she told him in a still breathless voice. "You can do that anytime you want to. I haven't had an orgasm like that even once in my life."

"Orgasm?" Sabin asked drawing his brows together.

"Snake?" Gressen asked. What was a snake?

Caro laughed, the sound going a log ways to sooth him. "An orgasm is what you have when you," she hesitated seeming to think. "It's that amazing feeling you get when you are satisfied or you spill your seed when you have sex."

Sabin nodded with an odd smile as he looked over at Gressen. "It is when a male brings a female to completion then."

Gressen had never heard of their females screaming when the males brought them to completion. Had they just not said anything to protect their females, or did theirs not have that tendency? He needed to ask one of the older males.

"And what is a snake?" Gressen asked.

Caro smiled, but a shadow crossed her eyes. "They are a creature on our planet that is very long. They're also called a serpent. I'm not sure if you have anything like that here. I didn't mean it as any sort of insult. It's just that very few of our males have long tongues, and I'm not sure that even those few have one as generous as yours."

Gressen just nodded, making sure he showed no hint of it bothering him. While it didn't, he knew from his brother that when something puzzled him, he often had a displeased expression. He didn't want Caro to think she'd upset him.

"It's yours and Sabin's turn now," Caro said, her smile turned sultry as she rolled over and crawled up Sabin's body.

"Our turn?" Sabin all but squeaked out. "We didn't think you were ready for anything more right now. We would never have pushed you for anything you weren't willing to do, Caro."

"The two of you have gotten me so hot and excited that I need you both now. Are you saying you don't want me anymore?" she asked narrowing her eyes and sitting back on her heels.

"No! Suns, no. We do, sweet Caro, but…" Sabin trailed off looking over to Gressen with a helpless look widening his eyes.

Gressen drew in a breath. Was she really ready to commit to them? He'd prayed and wished for this moment, but now that it was here, he couldn't quite believe it was true. He'd expected it to take much longer with both of them being Levassians. Unlike Caro, Della had mated with one of her own kind, so there hadn't been as much for her to get used to, and Kane had made the commitment and integration much easier.

"Sweet Caro, we want you more than the combined heat of the two suns," he told her. "We didn't want to rush you or appear immature in our haste."

Caro lowered her eyes, her long lashes covering them so that he couldn't tell what she was thinking. Had she changed her mind now that he'd interrupted the moment? It was best that he had if she really wasn't sure.

"You're not rushing me. I would not have started the process by teasing Sabin if I wasn't ready. I want you, Gressen." She lifted her eyes and stared directly into his eyes. "I want both of you. Right now. If you don't want me, tell me and I'll go. I would never say anything derogatory about either of you if you've changed your mind. We just didn't fit together. I understand."

Gressen lunged for Caro when she started to climb off of Sabin, toward the edge of the bed. "Caro, no. We do want you. I think we've made that more than clear. If you are ready, then we are honored. I've held my brother back some as I didn't want to overwhelm you. Please, don't see that as reluctance. There is none where you are concerned, sweetness."

The way Caro's face lit up chased away all the niggling doubts as to her readiness to commit to them. He was sure his face beamed back at her. His brother's was almost silly with such a huge smile on his narrow face.

"Um, Gressen?" Caro began. "Have either of you had anal sex before?"

Chapter Seven

Shock and just a little fear colored Gressen's face an odd blue-green. What had she said? If they hadn't had anal sex before, she needed to explain about lubrication and preparing her. God, she hadn't thought about that. Maybe she should have waited and talked to Della to see if Veran had known what to do. Why had she gotten so aroused waking up between them like that? She shouldn't have acted on it as she'd done. She was never spontaneous like that. Always before, she'd thought things through before initiating anything.

"Caro, our males have never, um, been attracted to each other. I understand this is something that your males often practiced back on Earth, but we are not inclined to that. Is this something females do to your males back on Earth, as part of sharing sex?" Gressen asked her.

Caro blinked so slowly she was surprised her eyelids even made it back up. Did he think she wanted to do that to him? That would sure explain the look of shock and a little fear on poor Sabin's face.

"N–no. I mean, yes. Some males on Earth were inclined that way. They preferred male partners, and there were some females who preferred female partners, but no. I didn't mean I wanted to, um, perform that to you and Sabin." Caro had to bite her tongue to keep from laughing when their expressions switched to relief quickly followed by carefully neutral looks.

"Then I'm not clear on what you were asking. Can you clarify your statement?" Gressen's body relaxed as he leaned against the steel and what appeared to be leather from the *aragus* creature they'd seen on their trip from their downed ship.

"I, um, was referring to me. I wondered if you knew the basics of having anal sex with a female. If not, we need to go over some things so that it doesn't hurt me," she explained.

"Ah, brother. She is talking about preparing her so that she doesn't feel pain during the act of taking both of us at the same time." Sabin smiled, looking over to her. "We've never performed this before, but have researched it when your Della took her mates. Our males began sharing many cycles ago when our females were so few."

"We don't know if those males actually shared anal sex with their female mate since it is a sensitive subject. It would be inappropriate to ask such of those still living," Gressen explained.

"That's fine. There's always a first time for everyone, but we should talk about it and be sure we all understand the, um, mechanics of it." Suddenly Caro felt awkward and unsure when before she'd been fine.

"We have the lubrication that Veran suggested, and have thoroughly discussed it with him to assure we would not hurt you should you agree to this with us." Sabin smiled before climbing off the bed and walking over to where her bathroom unit was hidden within the wall. He pressed his hand to it and when it emerged, he disappeared inside for a second, then reemerged with a bottle of something.

Holding it up, Sabin nodded at the bottle. "This is luster oil. It is a biologic extract from the luster plant native to our planet. Normally it is a medicinal oil we use to alieve some of the pain and discomfort of our elderly males' joints. It penetrates the skin to sooth those areas. I believe Veran said it also desensitized at first, but soon had a warm feeling that greatly enhanced Della's enjoyment."

"Um, TMI, Sabin." Caro cringed at knowing that much about Della without her telling Caro herself.

"TMI?" Gressen's brows knit together. "What does that mean?"

Caro laughed. "Too much information. It's a saying when someone overshares. Or, says something so personal that you really didn't want to know about that person. Like, maybe bathroom habits."

"Ah." Gressen laughed. "When Councilman Arak talks about how much he itches in that area that we hate to hear about."

Sabin made a disgusted face and shook his head. "Consider yourself lucky, brother. You only hear about it. I have to see it and treat it when he can't stand it any longer."

Caro couldn't stop the chuckle at both males' expressions. Seeing Gressen with anything other than a careful or neutral expression thrilled her. It gave him a much less imposing demeanor. Although she knew from how he treated her that he wasn't really a scowling male, it relieved her to know that he could actually tease and relax some.

"Well, now that we've completely destroyed the moment," she began. "I guess we should get up. I want to see Della and find out if anything new has happened regarding last night."

"Destroyed the moment? Did something we said cause you to change your mind?" Sabin asked.

"No. I just figured you wouldn't be interested in that now that we've talked all around it like we have. The mood or atmosphere is different now." She realized that she'd lost them. "You know. The romance and intimacy is gone."

Gressen and Sabin exchanged puzzled expressions, then turned back to her, still appearing confused. Maybe since they hadn't been around females, they didn't even know what romance or intimacy was. Caro closed her eyes and sighed. This was proving to be much more difficult than it should have been.

"I believe romance is something Kane talked about, but neither I nor Sabin understood what he meant. Veran seemed to understand. We will talk to Veran about it. Is it something we need to do?" Gressen asked.

Caro sighed and sat cross-legged on the bed. "Romance is a state of being, I guess. You're being romantic when you do something special and intimate for your partner. Like lighting candles around the room to make it feel cozy and, well, intimate. Do you understand intimate?"

"Yes," Gressen said. "It is affection and a special closeness. Our males who had females kept their females close, keeping their relationship intimate between them."

"That's pretty good. Not sure about sequestering their females, but I get it. Now romance is the act of getting to that state of intimacy. It is sort of the attitude you have when you are becoming intimate. You snuggle with each other and hold hands and give each other little gifts or pamper each other with massages or foot rubs. Does that help?" Caro wasn't sure she was getting her point across. Even with the programs, some expressions and words just didn't match up.

"So we should give you gifts and wrap our arms around you more often," Sabin said with a smile. "What sort of gifts do you require?"

"No, no. I'm not saying you have to give me gifts. That's just one way some people on Earth got romantic with each other. You don't have to do any of that. That's what makes it romantic." She sighed. "It's the little things you do just to make your partner happy or smile. It could be picking a wild flower and tucking it behind her ear for no reason, or fixing their favorite dish, or giving them a hug just because you feel like it."

"That should be very easy for us to do since seeing you smile or hearing you laugh pleases us very much," Gressen told her.

Caro knew she was blushing. Her face felt like a griddle ready for batter. It had been a long time since anyone had been able to elicit that sort of reaction from her. She'd already blushed at least twice since she'd been on this planet.

"That's so sweet, Gressen. That's something you'd do with romance. Say sweet things." She smiled at the male.

"So if I were to do this," Sabin moved her hair off one shoulder and kissed her neck where it curved into her shoulder before trailing his tongue up to the back of her ear. "It would create this romance and, perhaps, intimacy as well?"

Caro's gasp and shiver must have answered Sabin's question since Gressen got in on the seduction by brushing the backs of his long thick fingers across her nipples, then licking the ends of his fingers and rubbing the wet tips across her nipples. She shivered again and moaned as the cooler air awakened the nerves in her breasts making her taut buds protrude in reaction.

"I think you've got it now, guys." Caro let them slowly lower her back to the bed. "I believe you've recreated that spell."

* * * *

The two males drove her crazy with their mouths and fingers. While she'd been with two men before, this was entirely different. Not because they were physically different from the men on Earth, though that might play into things later, but because they really cared about pleasing her more than themselves. It was different because they weren't threatened by her knowledge, and allowed her to show them what she knew.

Caro had never been around males who weren't egotistical and arrogant to some extent until she'd met the males on Levasso. So far, she had yet to come across one who felt superior to anyone else. Even with Gressen's position over Veran, he never appeared to look down on him or treat him differently, other than when they were in their security roles. Veran showed no resentment or dissatisfaction with his subordinate place.

Gressen had an air of authority when working, or a situation like the night before occurred, but he didn't carry it all the time, even though he always appeared competent and secure in his abilities. Sabin wasn't quite as controlled as his brother, and tended to wear more of his personality openly for everyone to see how he felt at any given time. Still, he had a quiet competence that made her feel safe and secure, just like Gressen.

Caro's thoughts quickly disintegrated as the two males worshiped her body, their initially hesitant touches slowly becoming bolder. It took more and more strength to resist reaching for them when she wanted to allow them to explore her body and learn what turned her on.

"Gressen, Sabin. God, you're driving me crazy. It feels so good the way you touch my breasts," she told them.

"Shh, sweet Caro. We're going to take very good care of you." Gressen sucked in a nipple, rolling it with his talented tongue.

Sabin massaged her calves, dropping light kisses here and there with an occasional nip that stung until he licked the small hurt. His fingers were much smoother than his brother's. Gressen's fingers were callused, as well as the heels of his hands. The added stimulation when he rubbed them across her breasts sent tingles all down her spine. She swore she could feel his touch on her clit.

"Gressen, I can smell how much she wants us. It is the sweetest of aromas." Sabin spread Caro's legs and leaned down.

"Please, don't tease me. I need you both. I want you inside of me, Gressen." Caro was slowly losing control as she squirmed between them.

I'm going to explode if they don't take me soon. I've never needed anything as much as I need them to fuck me.

"We want you so aroused that there is no pain, Caro. Only pleasure," Sabin breathed against her pussy.

"I'm there. I swear, I'm already there. Please, guys. I ache for you."

Gressen's growl startled her, but she forgot all about it when Sabin lay on his back and Gressen rolled her on top of him.

"Help us take care of you, Caro. Show Sabin what to do so that we don't cause you pain," Gressen told her, his voice deepened.

"You won't hurt me, Sabin. Let me." Caro straddled the male's body, thankful that, as large as they were, her unusual height as a female gave her an advantage in being able to slowly lower her body down until the tip of his dick rubbed at her pussy slit.

When she pressed down so that the crown breached her opening, Sabin groaned, saying something she didn't understand. His fingers dug into her hips as she slowly slid down his shaft until he hit her cervix. The bump pinched, but Caro loved it. Not many men were endowed enough to be able to tap a cervix on the long torso of a tall woman. While it would send her into fiery orgasm after orgasm doggy style, or even in the missionary position, with her on top, she'd have to be careful not to relax too much or he'd really hurt her.

Once Gressen was ready to take her ass, she'd be okay lying over Sabin's chest. For now, she rode him with abandon, thrilling at his groans and what she assumed was curses in his language. Though he continued to dig his fingers into her hips, Sabin didn't once try and take over control of her careful strokes.

"Sabin, the sight of your cock sliding in and out of her pussy is amazing. My dick is twitching each time you disappear inside of her." Gressen crawled around behind Caro and rubbed his thick shaft between her ass cheeks.

"Yes!" she hissed out. "Please, Gressen, I need you inside of me, too."

"Lean down, sweetness. Sabin, be still until I'm inside of her. I don't want to hurt her." Gressen's hands smoothed down her back and over her ass.

She moaned when he squeezed her ass cheeks several times. Then his hands disappeared only to return to smear the oil Sabin had retrieved from her bath unit down the crease of her ass. It felt warm, unlike the lube that was used on Earth. Unless someone took the time to run hot water over the tube, it was always cold. This wasn't. How had he managed to warm it without her noticing?

"How am I doing, Caro? Kane said to use a lot. Tell me when you think it is enough," he said.

Before she could urge him to add more, he pressed against her hole with his finger and the warm oil. He didn't push his finger all the way in, but retreated only to return with more of the substance until her back passage allowed his finger deeper and deeper without a lot of effort on his part.

"That's amazing. It's so warm and tingly. It doesn't feel like you've used very much at all, but you're not having any trouble fucking me with your finger, are you?" she asked.

"No, the oil is doing its job and seeping into your tissues to relax them, and the warmth is part of what feels so good to stiff, painful joints." He added more oil and another finger.

"God, that's tight." She wasn't sure about two of his massive fingers, but as he slowly applied pressure, she opened for him so that it wasn't long until he slid in and out fairly easily.

"Are you okay, Caro? Is it too much?" Gressen asked.

"No. It's fine now. Your fingers are so large. With Sabin inside of me, it feels as if nothing more will fit, and you're cock is larger than your two fingers." Caro was beginning to worry.

"It will be fine, Caro. If it isn't, then we will stop. Just tell us so that we don't cause you pain or harm. That would kill us, sweet Caro." Gressen removed his fingers and added more of the oil.

The next sensation she had was of pressure as Gressen pressed his well-oiled cockhead against her back hole and pressed. He slipped some at first, but once he was able to breach the opening, he had better control.

"Caro? Say something, sweetness," Sabin coaxed. "I can feel you stiffening up all over. That isn't a good thing from what Veran told us. Relax."

"Hard to relax," she managed to pant out. "Pinches, takes my breath."

The pain was a bit more than a pinch, but she knew it would ease once Gressen's cock made it past the muscular rings at her entrance. The getting past it was the hard part. Caro buried her head against Sabin's chest and bit her lip to keep from crying out. She didn't want Gressen to stop, and she was sure if he knew she was having any pain at all, he would.

"Oh, suns, brother. She is so tight here. Is she okay? Can you tell? I feel as if I have to be hurting her." Gressen's strained voice had her doubling her effort to relax so that he wouldn't sense her unease.

I can do this. Della has talked about how good it felt to have both of her men inside of her. If she can do it, I can. I just wasn't thinking about how large their dicks were at the time.

Just when she was sure she was going to cave and cry out for Gressen to stop, the pinch flared, then disappeared as Gressen's shaft slid past the barrier and deeper into her dark depths. He stopped, leaning over her for a few seconds, laying his wet forehead on her back. His raspy breathing assured her that it hadn't been easy for him either.

"How do we do this, brother?" Sabin asked, his chest rumbling loud in her ear as he spoke.

"Somehow we are to take turns inside of her," Gressen told him.

"Gressen, you pull almost all the way back while Sabin pushes up, then he pulls back while you push in. It will be odd at first, but once you get into a rhythm, you'll get it." It took so much out of her to get that small explanation out.

She knew she'd have to help them initially, but once they understood and felt the rhythm, she could let them take control. When Gressen pulled back, dragging the ridge of his crown across tender tissues, Caro gasped in pleasure. She hadn't noticed that that part of their cockheads was much stiffer than the men's on Earth. That was going to feel amazing once the two men began fucking her between them for real.

Caro lifted off Sabin's dick while pushing back against Gressen's, filling her ass, then her cunt, over and over. It didn't take them long to find their stride, and Caro was able to let go and let them control everything. Sabin and Gressen worked together perfectly, sending waves of pleasure through her. Each wave built on the next until her ears rang with it, making everything around her sound far off.

Every once in a while, Sabin's cock would hit her cervix, ramping up the intense sensation building at her core. The pressure to come began to eat at her, teasing her with tingles of it, but never quite spilling over her. Caro knew from experience that if she reached for it, tried to capture it on her own terms, she'd end up exhausted with nothing but disappointment. But enduring the endless climb without trying to control it, drained her of the strength she needed to hold it off until the guys were ready.

"So close," Gressen ground out between clinched teeth.

"Hurry, brother. I can't hold on much longer. She's so wet and tight. My balls are tight enough to burst," Sabin wheezed.

"Her ass is hot enough to burn, brother. So tight, it almost hurts. Help our sweet Caro, brother. Give her the climax they talked of and we'll complete ourselves afterward."

Before what Gressen was saying could sink in to her fractured brain, Sabin pressed his hand between their bodies and rubbed a finger across her clit, letting the press of their bodies grind it against the tight bud. Almost instantly, Caro blew apart.

White-hot light exploded behind her closed eyelids as pleasure so rich and full that it almost hurt coursed through her veins and arteries. Burning its way through her body so that even areas that weren't usually invested in an orgasm felt the remnants of it. Heat seared her face and neck as she gasped for air, trying desperately to pull even one breath into her lungs.

Every muscle in her body clamped down and the faint cries of Gressen and Sabin penetrated the haze that had taken over her brain. It seemed to go on and on until finally, her body's strength failed her and she collapsed with ringing ears and ragged breaths onto Sabin’s heaving chest. None of them moved for so long, Caro wondered if they were dead. She knew she needed to get off Sabin so he could catch his breath, but with Gressen pressed against her back, she couldn’t move. Either lack of oxygen or complete exhaustion took over, and Caro fell asleep without ever opening her eyes. A soft grunt beneath her just before she drifted off made her giggle, but she wasn’t sure if it had only been in her mind, or if she’d giggled aloud.

Chapter Eight

Caro smiled as Della talked about all of the changes the council was making. Her friend had grown and blossomed in her role as a sort of ambassador or liaison between the council and those from Earth. Major John Lance would have been the obvious human to step into that role, but the council didn't trust him or most of the males since they'd kept so much from them in the beginning. They'd initially gotten off on the wrong foot, but had soon reconciled with the people of Levasso. They had agreed that it was only natural to be suspicious of each other at first, and the Major had the humans' wellbeing on his shoulders.

Kane Dancing Bear, one of Della's mates, had been the next choice, but he insisted he wasn't a negotiator or good with politics. He recommended Della since so much of the issues to be decided revolved around the females. Who better to take their case to the council than a female?

"I just don't want there to ever be a misunderstanding like that again. If you hadn't found out what was going on, that poor male would have been killed, and none of us the wiser, possibly being the one to cause the next death." Della shivered.

"You're the one who is going through all of the rules and stuff to weed out the dangerous ones," Caro reminded her. "I wouldn't wish that on my worst enemy. I don't know how you can stand going over all of that. It has to be boring reading."

Della giggled. "Between you and me, some of it is almost comical it's so wild. I have to really fight to keep from bursting out laughing when they read some of them to me."

Caro loved the light dancing in Della's eyes. Veran and Kane were so good to her. They catered to her as if she were the very air they breathed. She wanted that. Desperately.

Looking over her shoulder, she watched as Gressen and Veran talked together across the large common room. Kane was playing with something Veran had given him to learn to use. Sabin was at the clinic or hospital that he worked. She wished they were both home more. They each had such important jobs that they were often gone for long periods of time. It left her with little to do since they hadn't yet worked out suitable duties or jobs for females yet.

"What about jobs, Della? When are they going to let us have something to do? You're busy with them, but the rest of us are dying of boredom." Caro finally interrupted her friend.

"I know. I've given them a long list of things we know how to do and have done back on Earth. I talked to all the women to add their jobs to the list as well. They are going over the list to pick out what they would feel comfortable allowing us to do," Della told her, making a face when she said the word "allowed."

"I don't know why I'm even worrying over it. It's not like I have any experience in anything other than wearing clothes and smiling at a camera." Caro sighed and leaned back against the comfortable chair.

"I guess it gets pretty lonely here during the day when everyone is out. I'm sorry, Caro. I really hadn't thought about it. I guess I expected that someone would be here all the time."

"I don't need babysitting, Della. I just need something to do. There aren't even any magazines or books to read."

"Maybe I can ask if you can come to the council's rooms with me," she suggested.

Caro smiled. "That would really be nice. I like learning new things. There would be a lot of new things to learn there, I'm sure."

Della continued telling her about some of the things she'd encountered while going each day. Caro thought about how wonderfully the guys treated her when they made love each evening.

They hadn't slept with her since the first night when they'd all fallen asleep in a pile like puppies. The next morning, they'd been gone, but had left a sweet note saying they couldn't wait to see her when she rose for the day.

They'd tiptoed around each other for a few days as if afraid to say anything lest they upset the other. The uncomfortable atmosphere dissipated once they met up in her room at night, but was back the next morning.

Thankfully the tension between the three of them eased a little more each day. Caro just wasn't sure where they were headed. Not knowing how they truly felt about her and their relationship left a sour taste in her mouth. She didn't expect them to ask her to be their mate or anything, but she did think they might give her some hint of their feelings.

"How are the three of you getting along?" Della asked out of the blue.

"What? Oh, we're fine. They are very good to me. Sabin is quiet and Gressen is a little stiff, but they both treat me well." Caro avoided looking directly at the other female.

"I got the feeling that you were becoming an, um, threesome. Veran had gotten the idea that you had agreed to be mates," Della said with a slight frown.

"What? Why would he think that?"

Della shrugged. "I'm not sure. Maybe he talked with Sabin or Gressen and got the impression they were going to ask you or something."

Caro searched her friend's face, the feeling that Vella wasn't telling her everything too strong to ignore. Why would she keep something from her? It didn't make sense. She needed to talk to Gressen and Sabin, instead of letting things continue as they were. Maybe they were fine with having sex at night and acting like nothing was different during the day, but Caro wanted more than that. She needed more.

What is wrong with me? First, I didn't want to get involved if all I was going to be was a baby factory. Now I'm upset because they haven't treated me any differently now that we're having sex. I don't even want to be mated yet. Do I?

She rubbed her face, tired of the constant tangle of emotions in her head. It was all of the empty hours on her hands. She had nothing to do except dwell on things, blowing them up into something they weren't.

"Sweetness, are you tired? Does your head ache? Maybe we should retire early so you can get some rest." Gressen's sudden appearance next to her made her jump.

"Oh, you startled me. I didn't hear you walk up." Caro tried to slow her heart down. "I'm fine, Gressen. Della and I have been talking about all the changes she is helping to make by working with the council."

"We are all very grateful she agreed to help bridge our differences so we are able to interact without adverse issues arising. Already many of the males seem much more relaxed with the threat of death lifted from their minds." Gressen touched her shoulder with a small caress before withdrawing his hand.

Veran sat on the edge of the chair next to Della, holding one of her hands in both of his while Kane stood behind her, running his hands through her hair. They looked so happy and peaceful that Caro had to fight to keep from crying.

"You know, I am a little tired. I think I will head to bed early." She turned to Gressen. "There's no need for you to cut your evening short just to escort me to my room. Stay and talk more with Kane and Veran. Della, I'll talk to you tomorrow to find out what more you've managed to do." Caro winked at her friend in hopes it would ease some of the speculation in her eyes.

"Of course, I'll walk you back. I can resume my discussions with my friends another time." Gressen stepped back to allow her to stand.

"I'll find you tomorrow as soon as I return, Caro." Della waved as her mates pulled her to her feet as well.

The short walk back to their dome area was made in silence. She hated the uneasy stillness between them, but didn't know what to do about it. She didn't want to bring anything up for fear they would feel trapped into doing or saying something they really didn't mean. She didn't want to feel obligated to agree with something until she was sure about her feelings.

And I'm a fool for pretending to myself that I'm not already a little in love with them. What more could I ever want in a marriage, mating, or whatever it is? They treat me like a queen. They always look to me for my approval, and constantly worry about my wellbeing.

But was it out of fear of reprisal if something happened to her, or she said that she wasn't happy? Did they really enjoy her company and want to do things for her? How would she ever know how they really felt when every male on the planet wanted a mate to have children with? What made her special to them that they would have picked her, out of a thousand females? Or would they have even picked her in the first place?

The more she thought about it, the more confused and uncomfortable she became. Caro really had too much time on her hands. She needed a hobby if not a job.

"Do you need something for your head or to rest, Caro? You look as if you don't feel well. I've called Sabin to come check on you," Gressen said. The concern on his face gave her hope that he cared for her in a more special way, and not just a female in his care.

"Thank you, Gressen, but I'm fine. I didn't realize that you had called Sabin to leave work. I really just want something to do so that I don't feel so worthless and bored. I wish the council would hurry up and make up their minds on some positions we could fill."

"I do not understand this need you feel to work. Many of the other females do not push to have something to do. They seem content to visit and relax. Is there something we're not doing or providing that you need? Whatever it is, we will take care of it."

"Take care of what, brother?" Sabin strode toward them at a fast pace. "Caro, are you unwell? What is bothering you?"

"I'm fine, Sabin. I think Gressen is just picking up on my frustration. I need something to do. I want to work and help provide for myself. You've given me everything—clothes, food, shelter—and I've done nothing to give back."

"Sweet Caro, you need not worry about such things. We will always provide for you."

"It's not about needing things, Gressen. It's about needing to feel needed for something. I don't like doing nothing but sitting here all day. I want to do something productive, or I'm going to waste away and become a mindless doll who can't think for themselves." She turned to Sabin. "Can't you understand that?"

Sabin slowly nodded his head. He looked over to his brother with a grim expression. "Brother, I do not believe she is happy with us. Maybe we should…"

"She chose us. We are a mated family now," Gressen interrupted. He turned to Caro and looked down at her with what she could only describe as panic on the big male's face. "We have already disappointed you?"

Caro hadn't gotten past Gressen's words that they were a mated family now, or the unusual expression of panic that even now filled his eyes.

A mated family? Why did he believe that? They don't sleep with me. Yes, I've had sex with them every night for the last week, but we haven't talked about anything permanent. Did I miss something?

"What? No, you haven't disappointed me. Why would you think that?" Caro struggled to keep up with what was going on while those words swam in her head.

"You are wishing to do something because you are bored and unhappy. We aren't meeting your needs. What can we do to correct this? What do you need from us?" Gressen asked.

"Nothing, Gressen. You and Sabin do everything in the world for me, but what I want is to actually *do* something worthwhile. I have never been comfortable leading a life of luxury. Even when I was modeling back on Earth, and could have spent any downtime I had just lazing around a pool, I kept busy with other things. I worked in a soup kitchen to feed the homeless, or took a group of girls who didn't have anything to the mall to buy a cute outfit and get their hair fixed." Caro could tell they were still confused.

And why wouldn't they be? They hadn't really had females around them the entirety of their lives. There were no homeless to feed or teenage girls with dysfunctional families who needed an older sister to talk to and to spoil them just a little. What could she possibly do here in a Utopian type of society?

"You enjoy helping others," Sabin finally said.

Caro looked up and gave the male a sad smile. "Yeah. I don't think you have anyone here who is sad or lonely who could use my friendship though. You live a contented and productive life."

Gressen heaved out a strangled sigh and stiffened his shoulders with his head lifted. "If we can't provide for your happiness, we have no choice but to release you from our mate bond. You are welcome here for as long as you wish to remain. We will make sure your needs are addressed, but we will not force you to interact with us if you do not wish to."

"Here is your room, Caro. Rest well. If you should need anything, you know you can call on us," Sabin added.

The wistful look in his eyes just before he turned and walked over to his room pulled at her heart. What had she done?

Chapter Nine

Sabin stood up from working at his desk and stretched. He'd been working on the same thing for thirty minutes now. He couldn't concentrate with thoughts of losing Caro on his mind. He needed to focus on assuring they had the supplies they needed to keep on hand at the clinic. They rarely had need for much, but they'd been known to have devastating storms with large casualties, especially those who lived outside the city.

Then there were the infrequent aragus attacks. Most of their males weren't trained to handle the dangerous creatures with their tough skin. They were nearly impossible to kill, and only those trained to fight them were able to escape with minor injuries. Moreover, since the addition of the humans to their city, there had been several accidents to deal with. The males tended to be curious and get into trouble easily.

While they didn't have these events occur frequently, there were minor things to care for, and they always had at least two males scheduled for health exams each day. Part of his duties was to make sure residents were informed of their health days, and assigning a healer to check them. Prevention was how they'd avoided mass illnesses and diseases in their population. The hardest to care for were the field workers who lived outside the city. They didn't like coming into the city to the clinic.

The field workers who had their own community outside were a proud population of males intent on keeping their race fed. With the loss of about ten percent of their males each year, first to age so that they could no longer work, and then to death, the number of

Levassians able to work and continue to provide for the communities had increased the amount of work for those still able to contribute.

The elder males needed more frequent checks and because it was difficult for them to get out and to the clinic. Their healers went out to them. It would be his turn to make those visits in a few days. Sometimes it took him three or four days to complete his list, simply because the males wanted to visit, talk about the past, and how much they missed the females. It meant he often spent much more time with each of them than was necessary.

Some of the healers didn't have the desire or inclination to spend the extra time with the elders. Sabin felt that their emotional and mental health was just as important to their physical health when many of his colleagues didn't subscribe to that belief. To them, it was a waste of time to cater to their mental wanderings.

He'd often wished he could direct some of the much younger males to spend time with the elders each day and listen to their stories. Not only would it give the older males company and a feeling of worth by regaling the younger males with tales of the way things used to be, and how they'd come to be the strong, prosperous race they were, but it would teach the young males the importance of their history. It would also show them the need to continue the traditions and rules that had kept them alive all these years. It would instill in them a respect for those who'd come before them as well.

Unfortunately, no one else thought it was a worthwhile project, and the council had rejected it. It vindicated him to some degree that his brother had stood by his side, believing he was correct, despite many of his coworkers agreeing with the council.

Instead, he'd been obsessing about Caro and what had happened days before. Since that night, they'd seen little of her. She spent a lot of her time with Della when the other female was home, and the rest of the time she kept to her room. He'd worried she might venture out on her own some. Though he knew no one would dare hurt her, he was afraid someone would lure her from their home. Maybe it would happen sooner or later, but he wasn't prepared to lose her presence right away. Their home held her scent in it. He didn't want to dread the day it dissipated after she'd gone.

Sabin crossed the room and pressed his hand on the wall next to a supply berth. A rectangle section of the wall thinned so that he could see outside of the clinic and onto the street.

This time of day there were always males walking up and down to their destinations after having taken a mid-day meal. After they finished eating, they rested for an hour, then returned to work. He'd remained at the clinic to eat and rest this time. He let the others go instead, preferring to remain since Caro had changed her mind about them. He couldn't bear to go home knowing she wouldn't want to spend time with him while he was there.

What had changed her mind? When she'd accepted them into her body, both he and his brother had been overjoyed that she'd accepted their mating. For her to suddenly decide that they were not able to fulfill her needs was devastating. It hurt on a level he'd never experienced before. What could he do to take away the sad, lost look in her eyes that had slowly grown over the last weeks?

Sabin didn't expect to change her mind, but if he could somehow give her something she needed, maybe she wouldn't hurry to leave their home. Just having her there gave him a small slice of peace that had never been there before. Even Gressen seemed much less stoic with her around.

He thought about what she'd said about feeling needed and worthwhile. He didn't understand about a soup kitchen, but she said she fed the homeless from this soup kitchen. It wasn't something they'd ever had that he knew of. None of the peoples of his race were without shelter and food. It was there for everyone when they needed it. No one took more than they needed, and everything was always the best possible so there was no choosing. They had artisans who created special pieces for the love of their craft and would trade for them. Sometimes they wished a special door for their home, or maybe they wanted a special sweet or meal made that they couldn't make. Everyone always benefited in a manner that they wanted.

Since they had no children on Levasso, the notion of a child without a caring family to take them places and do things with them didn't make sense to him either, but one of the things all of the humans had talked about was the overpopulation of their world, and the sickening amount of violence and danger from their own kind. The idea that children had been abused and ignored was unfathomable to them.

Caro wanted to do something that helped their people as she'd done for hers. He valued that about her and thought much more of her for that reason. But what could she do like that on their world?

Then it hit him. The elders. They were lonely and few spent time with them. She could visit them, take them treats, and tell them about her world while they told her about theirs. Why hadn't he thought about that sooner? Maybe they wouldn't have lost her if he hadn't been so convinced she didn't need to work.

Sabin couldn't wait until his shift was over with now. He wanted to talk to Gressen before they approached Caro with the idea. It wasn't that he thought his brother wouldn't approve, it was that he wanted his brother's input about some of what she could do, and he wanted to be sure his brother was a part of the possible solution. The only worry he had was that she wouldn't like the idea of talking with a lot of older males. Maybe there was another female who might like to go with her. Then she wouldn't be alone. At last, he had something to look forward to after long days of worrying over their loss of sweet Caro.

* * * *

Nothing held her attention for long. Caro wanted to go out and explore, but knew it wouldn't be a good idea to go alone. Gressen and Sabin had both assured her she was safe from harm in their city, but

Caro didn't know her way around and there were too many males without their own female to risk attracting unwanted attention.

She still couldn't believe she'd insulted the two males as she had. Caro was so ashamed of her behavior. She didn't know how to tell them she was sorry without needing to go into a long explanation over what she meant and how it wasn't their fault she wasn't happy. After learning from Della that she'd essentially married the two males when she'd started having sex with them, Caro was afraid to do or say anything that might be misunderstood.

If she were honest, Caro had to admit that for a few seconds, she'd been secretly excited at the idea that she was mated to Sabin and Gressen until she remembered that she'd also kind of divorced them as well. Without even knowing it, she'd had a little part of what she'd wanted in the first place, the closeness and rightness of a relationship with the two males.

Della had explained that until she gave them the signal that it was fine to freely touch and hold her, they would remain attentive, but refrain from touching her too much around others. They were following her signals in an effort to please her. Caro choked back a sob. Why hadn't she been more open with Della to begin with and learned all of this before she'd screwed it all up?

Now she rarely saw them. They worked long hours and Sabin didn't even return to the house for the mid-day meal anymore. She'd gotten used to his presence for that hour and a half. They'd talk about the planet with Sabin giving her some of the history of the place before he returned to work.

I'm so stupid! I had it all right in front of me and blew it. Now I'm back where I started, alone and feeling useless.

What could she do now? Avoiding them all together really wasn't working, and if she were honest, was childishly immature. She was better than this. She needed to open up a conversation and be honest with the two males who'd been nothing but good to her.

Having made up her mind to make the first move, Caro jumped up from where she'd been sitting in the common room and immediately became dizzy. She grabbed for the chair's arm to steady herself and caught her breath. Gradually, the whirling feeling in her head died down and she was able to walk across the room without it returning.

What had that been about? She'd never had that happen to her before. Maybe she'd been sitting too long in one place without moving, and jumping up as she had might have caused it.

Just as she reached the food prep area to get a glass of saufass juice, the front door slid open with a soft whoosh. Though she knew it was about time for the two males to return, it still startled her. The domed home was always quiet when there was no one there but her.

"Caro?" Sabin's voice as he walked from the entrance into the common room sounded odd.

She carried her glass from the food prep area and hurried out to see if something was wrong. Had Gressen gotten hurt?

"I'm here, Sabin. Is something wrong?"

His face brightened in direct proportion to the light in his dark green eyes. It made the golden circle around the pupil almost glow. Caro stopped just in front of him, trying not to hold her breath at the way he looked at her. She felt devoured until he spoke.

"Nothing is wrong, sweetness. I wanted to see you and wasn't sure if you were in your room or not. How are you feeling this day?" he asked as he led the way to the common room to sit.

"Um, I'm fine. Were you busy at the clinic today?"

Caro wasn't sure where this was going. Though they'd often exchange pleasantries when the males first returned home in the evenings, this seemed different somehow. Sabin appeared far less ill at ease than he normally did, and an air of expectation hung between them. What did it mean?

"No more so than normal. I will be going out to do my rounds with our elders for their health visits in the next few days, so I've been preparing my packs and reviewing their records." Sabin smiled.

"What about you, Caro? Did you find anything to pass the time today?"

She sighed and shook her head. "I worked on the information unit to learn more about the city and try to learn the names of things around me. I learned that the purple flowers I saw on our way into the city were called *listras*, and that they're poisonous. If the aragus loves them so much, which is why they stay so close to the city, why don't you get rid of the plant so that the creature won't be a danger near the city? You could even plant the things farther away to keep them there." It had been bugging her ever since she'd read about the flower being a favorite of the nasty animal.

"That is a very intelligent observation, Caro. We've tried to destroy the field of flowers many times, but they quickly grow back. Burning them and poisoning them hasn't deterred their growth. The only time we can burn them is when the wind isn't blowing in the direction of the town or our crops. The smoke is just as toxic to us as the actual plant and flower." Sabin had sat in the chair across from hers and was leaning forward with his elbows resting on his knees.

"Goodness. That is terrible. There just seems like there would be some way to destroy them," she mused as she thought more on it.

"The idea of transplanting the plants in another area is actually a good suggestion. We haven't thought of that, as far as I know. We did try pulling them up and destroying them that way, but we have to wear protective clothing, and with our two suns, it becomes very hot very quickly in them."

Caro nodded. She'd keep thinking about it and maybe she could come up with a solution to that problem. It would be something she could do to help with a challenge facing the Levassians. She almost laughed aloud. It would help her fellow humans as well. They lived with the inhabitants of the planet now, too.

"Maybe I can think of something else that will work." Caro sipped at her juice. "Why is it that you think your job as a healer isn't as important as any of the other jobs?"

Caro couldn't believe she'd just asked that. What had come over her? "I'm sorry. That's none of my business. I shouldn't have said anything."

She stood up to go to her room, but Sabin stood up as well and touched her shoulder. "No. It's okay. Please don't go."

Caro's face felt as if a hot blast of air from the exhaust of a bus had touched it. Why did she blurt things out like that around them? She'd never done such a thing until she'd met Sabin and Gressen.

"I—I'm sorry, Sabin. It's just that a healer back on Earth was treasured as one of the most important callings, um, professions there was. It takes a lot to become one, and even more to be a good one," she said.

"Among our people, healers are who they are by their genetic makeup. We are born with an affinity to know what is wrong and how to heal it. The devices we use are more like an extension of our abilities to heal. They wouldn't work in the hands of anyone without that inborn genetic material," he told her.

"That is even more amazing. I don't understand why that doesn't make you valued above all others," she said, shaking her head.

"Because we have no choice, and therefore have not earned our place in our society. We don't have to study or train like our security and our workers in the field. They both have to learn how to do their jobs, and there is always the opportunity to excel or fail." Sabin seemed to struggle to get his point across, his mouth twisting even as his eyes closed in concentration. "We did not have to strive and struggle to accomplish our positions. We merely had to reach an age where we were able to focus the talent of healing."

"I still say that because of that unique ability, you should be considered the greatest among you. What happens if no one is ever born with it again? Then you would be in tough straights, Sabin." Caro stopped and covered her mouth with one hand. "I—I guess that is what has been happening since you've not had children in so many years. I'm sorry. I just can't open my mouth without something completely inappropriate falling out."

She once again tried to walk away, but Sabin actually wrapped his hand around her upper arm to stop her. It was the first time either male had actually used their will on her to keep her from doing something. Even in bed, they were so careful with their touches.

"Please, don't go. You've said nothing wrong. There is no secret or bitterness over our situation. We are saddened by it, but have long made our peace with our eventual demise. We tried, at first, to locate females of similar make up to mate, but as you know, that led to more trouble by allowing other races to try and take over our resources through subterfuge, and by bargaining with promises of compatible females." Sabin's smile appeared so sad to her.

"But now you have us, who basically fell from the skies like a gift from heaven. You have hope again," Caro said softly.

"Yes, there is hope, but we are all still cautious to truly believe. We desperately want to have mates and young once again, but it isn't in our hearts to force or coerce your females to choose us. We will stumble all over ourselves to catch your attentions and try to please you, but it has to be your choice in the end, or it would be a bitter sweet victory." Sabin slowly pulled her a little closer, but quickly dropped his hand from her arm when he realized what he was doing.

Horror then fear widened his eyes, but when she didn't show any indication that she was upset or bothered by it, Sabin's expression relaxed even as his shoulders dropped with the relief of the tension.

"It would please us even if you choose only your own race of males as you will still produce young who will laugh and play and bring joy to our hearts just the same. Maybe years down the line, those young will grow up to choose mates, and the cycle will begin again. Levassians may eventually die out completely, but a new race will still exist here, and before we do die, we will have enjoyed the fruits of an alliance with your people. What more can any species, race, or being ask?"

Caro's heart broke for Sabin and Gressen. More than that, it bled for the acquiescence of a proud people to their fate as they saw it. They'd fought against it, tried to beat it and negotiate it, and when nothing worked, they accepted that what was to be, was to be.

"There may never be a pure Levassian born again, Sabin, but there will be Levassian blood in many of them. Not all of my females will choose human males. You're males have shown them a better way of life, and many of them will want this new life. Della has chosen one of your males and will probably become pregnant before long since that is why we were chosen for the mission in the first place," Caro said.

"Thank you for that, sweet Caro. While we would all love to have a mate and maybe young, none of us will resent another their good fortune should it happen. We will all celebrate each new union and each new life as if it were our own," Sabin said giving her a soft kiss on her forehead. "Enough of this sadness you are showing. These are happy times, and Gressen and I may have a surprise for you. As soon as he arrives, we will discuss it with you."

Caro smiled. She loved surprises, but worried what it might be that they would need to discuss it together with her. A churning began in her stomach that she might have given them the wrong impression, and they had found her somewhere else to live. That would not be a good surprise at all, and Caro didn't know how she would be able to stand it if they were planning for her to leave.

Chapter Ten

The sound of the entrance opening broke the spell between her and Sabin just before Caro asked him what the surprise was. Gressen strode into the room with a smile on his face. She hadn't seen that from him in several days now. She prayed that his good humor wasn't based on something that would send her away. That would break her heart.

"Sweet Caro. It is good to see you in the common room. How are you doing this evening?" he asked, lightly brushing his lips against her hair.

"I'm well, Gressen. Sabin and I were just talking about, um, about the listra field where the aragus creatures like to eat." Caro knew she was babbling, but couldn't stop the nerves jumping around in her throat.

She had no right to want to take back the impression she'd given the two males that she wasn't happy with them, but she did. She'd never meant for them to think it was them she was unhappy with. It was her situation that had her so out of sorts with feelings of inadequacy. Yet once she'd set the thought into motion, the males had continued with it, giving her no chance to stop their assumptions since she hadn't realized they considered themselves mated to her. What could she possibly do about it now?

"That is an odd subject to be discussing, Sabin," Gressen said with a frown aimed at his brother.

"I was telling him about studying it on the information terminal and how I didn't understand why you didn't get rid of the flower so that nasty creature would stay farther away, and…" Caro stopped, shaking her head. "Sorry. I'm sure you aren't interested in my thoughts on that subject."

"No, sweetness. I am interested in any thoughts you have," Gressen said. "Come sit with us. Has Sabin told you of his idea?"

"Not just my idea, brother. Yours, too." Sabin's golden skin darkened at his face and neck.

"He said it was a surprise and that you would both tell me." Caro's heart felt as if it was choking her.

"You talked about the things you did back on your Earth that made you feel useful and needed. You couldn't think of anything here as you feel as if we have no real troubles that you could help with. That is not true," Gressen said. "We have many things that are not perfect here. We have our own shortcomings that plague us, and until you, sweet Caro, we never knew what to do about them. Now we do."

"I don't understand." Caro leaned forward, facing the two males sitting across from her now.

"With the lack of children to raise and help replenish our working males, we are constantly spending more and more of our time doing the jobs that used to be handled by many more. Once we each worked only six of our sun's hours each day, and only four days at a time. Now, our males are growing older and more and more are having to shorten the hours they work, or the days they work until they eventually can no longer function well enough to safely perform their duties," Gressen explained.

"For those who work in the fields, their time is shorter due to the hard work they have keeping our people fed. Our security forces grow fewer and fewer as well," Sabin added.

"While your males are helping to ease that burden now, it does nothing for those of us who are no longer able to contribute." Gressen looked over at his brother.

"They feel worthless and a burden to the others. The younger males have no time to spend with their own fathers and grandfathers. Those who do have some time don't feel comfortable around the older males. So these males are alone and their knowledge is wasting away," Sabin explained.

"That is so sad. Aren't there programs where they can commune with each other and talk? Someone should set up a common area where they can meet daily just to be around others their ages. Those who can't get around as easily should have someone check on them periodically and visit for a while. I can't imagine how lonely and despondent they must get." Caro wanted to talk to someone about these older males' treatment.

"We've never seen it as a problem before. Sabin's talked about the need to have our younger males learn from them, which would help the older males feel important, but our council would not sanction it," Gressen told her.

"Why not?" Caro was enraged for the older males.

"They felt that the time lost working would make too large of an impact on our production and work levels." Sabin shrugged. "They are right, but it doesn't really mean it's wrong to make that difference."

"Won't they be old and alone one day?" Caro asked indignant that this council thought themselves immune to old age.

"Yes, in fact, several are already talking about it being their time to step down. It is a way of life they have grown to accept and expect. They know they will soon be part of the older male population with no purpose. Yet they still think only of the good of all, and not the few," Gressen said.

"That is what we've always called socialism, where the good of the many overrides the good of a few. It's okay to sacrifice a few people if it will help or save the majority of the people." Caro hurt for the older Levassians. "Many of us believe that saving even one person is worth the effort. Those in the majority should be able to take care of themselves and each other. The one alone should be helped back into the majority and safety. To focus only on those able to contribute something tangible is shortsighted and just plain wrong. Those older males have so much to offer. They might not remember how to do something they've been doing for years, or what they ate at last meal, but they will remember the history of your race and what worked and what didn't work. You could learn so much from their memories."

"We agree with you, Caro. That's why we would be forever grateful if you would consider starting some kind of program, as you call it, to help them. It would be a huge undertaking, but maybe there would be other females who would enjoy the challenge and interaction with our elders to help you," Gressen told her.

"Is this something that would help you to feel needed and make you happy?" Sabin asked, a look of pure hope brittle in his stance.

"Yes, Sabin. This is exactly what I would want to do. It would make me very happy to help these poor males. Gressen, you and your brother have made me so happy. I won't feel like a burden, eating your food and not contributing unless I had someone's young. It made me feel wanted and needed for nothing more than my ability to have a baby. It was what many of us forced to make the trip to another planet felt," she said.

"I don't understand." Gressen leaned forward this time.

"The men, um, males were chosen to go on the trip based on their abilities, such as to build, farm, or as a doctor—healer. The women, ah, females were only chosen if they could still have children, and for this trip, we had to be highly fertile. The males had no say in who they were paired with, and neither did the females. We didn't feel important for any other reason, and knew that many of the males would never have looked at us if we hadn't been forced on them." Caro looked down to find that she was wringing her hands in her lap. She stilled them.

"I can understand how you felt now, sweetness. I'm so sorry we also have made you feel this way," Gressen said, a soft smile belying the sadness in his eyes.

"We have never looked at you in that fashion, Caro. Yes, we would love to be blessed with a mate and maybe even young, but what makes you so special to us is your ability to see more than what we see. You have a kind heart and a strong spirit. Those are the things that make you beautiful in our eyes," Sabin told her.

"I'm sorry I misunderstood you the other night. And, I want you to know that I didn't suddenly decide that I didn't like being your mate. I didn't even know that I had made that step by sleeping with you. I thought we were enjoying each other, and never guessed that it meant more than that to you," she told them.

"We have not slept together, Caro." Sabin's confused expression was so funny that Caro burst out laughing.

"I'm sorry. In our language, we often call having sex, making love, as sleeping with each other. And actually, Sabin, we did sleep with each other that first time." She winked at him.

Once again, the golden male's skin darkened. She was sure it was a blush now. Gressen's face broke into a wide, unexpected smile.

"She caught you on that, my Brother."

"We are sorry about that, Caro. We knew better than to spend the night in your room, but after our love making, we were all exhausted, and neither Gressen nor myself woke until the day's beginning. We left as soon as we realized what we'd done." Sabin's words reminded her of what else she'd talked about with Della.

"Sabin, unlike your females, human females expect the male they choose to sl—um—have sex with, to sleep all night with them. Mated pairs on earth share a bed from their wedding night on. You did nothing wrong by staying all night. The only thing that would have been better was to wake up between the two of you, instead of alone the next morning."

Both males smiled broadly. Then Sabin's expression sobered. "Would you be willing to let us, I think the word is, court you again?"

Caro felt tears build behind her eyes. The burning sensation reminded her that she needed to swallow her pride and come clean with the two males. There was no way they only wanted her for her ability to have their young or be their mate. They had gone out of their way to find something that would make her happy, even if it didn't include them. That was love.

"I would be honored if you would allow me to choose you as my mates. I never meant to drive you away. I was just unsure of how you really felt about me. I'm sorry I doubted you." Caro stood up, trying to make the first step toward them, but Gressen beat her to it.

Caro found herself surrounded by Levassian male flesh—hot, hard male flesh. Sabin had her back covered, his thick dick rubbing from the top of her ass to her lower back while Gressen's male flesh pressed intimately into her abdomen. His rigid cock with its flared head elicited very naughty thoughts she was more than anxious to share.

"Does this mean you will continue to share my bed? Will you sleep all night with me?" she asked, tilting her head back so that she could see Gressen's face.

"No, Caro," he said.

Her heart thudded hard in her chest. She'd screwed everything up once again.

"It means that you will join us in our bed and sleep with us from now on. You are our mate and we are yours. It will be much easier to protect you between us, and allow us the pleasure of waking you with kisses and other things as well." Gressen winked at her.

Sabin nipped her neck just below her ear. "I can't wait to sample your sweet desire again, Caro. I've missed the taste of your skin just after you've climaxed."

Heat burned her cheeks and her neck at their sexy words. They had made the effort to learn from Veran and Kane what human females liked, and the words they used, which was much more than most human men had done back on Earth. The teenage boys taught each other how to get in a girl's pants, but not how to make her feel good before they got their own jollies. She prayed that the human males who'd lived through the crash wouldn't teach the males of Levasso their inadequacies and poor habits.

"You'll turn a lady's head talking like that," she whispered between them.

"Lady? Why would we turn her head?" Sabin asked.

Caro chuckled. They were too much fun. "Let me tell you about our planet in the seventeenth and eighteenth century. It was a time of knights, and ladies, and dragons. In fact, your aragus is a lot like our dragons were."

"This sounds more like a history lesson than it does a seduction, brother," Sabin said with a loud sigh.

"We will pretend to listen while we distract her with other things," Gressen replied.

Chapter Eleven

"Are you sure it's okay for me to be with you when you're going to be doing a medical exam?" Caro asked Sabin two days later.

"Yes, sweetness. I wouldn't have asked you along if it wasn't. We are almost there." Sabin carried a pack, and had refused to let Caro carry one as well.

Instead, she used one of the pretty lengths of material she'd gotten from Livitius at the commons area. She'd fashioned it into a sling bag of sorts and carried a few things she wanted with her. When Sabin had asked to carry it for her, Caro had pretended horror and informed him that it was a female's personal bag. Women on Earth carried them everywhere, and males only held them if the female needed her hands free for shopping or something. It had worked and he hadn't asked to carry it again.

"That is where several of our elder males live." Sabin pointed to a large domed home much like theirs but the colors were faded and the building material that formed it looked chipped.

"Why does it look so run down?" she asked.

Sabin stopped and looked at it before looking around at the other homes nearby that were in good shape. Flustered at the differences, Sabin didn't answer right away. Finally, he wiped his hands on his pant legs and sighed.

"I've never noticed it before. Evidently, no one has. I will make sure repairs are done immediately. I'm ashamed for you to have noticed this and I haven't."

"It's okay, Sabin. That's part of why I'm here. Now introduce me to these older males."

Sabin nodded but still didn't smile. Caro just rolled her eyes and followed him. He would get over it and relax once more. She'd slowly begun to learn to interpret their moods and what they meant. Right now, Sabin was embarrassed that she'd noticed something and he hadn't before. More than likely, he was also embarrassed that they had allowed their elder males to live in this fashion.

Sabin pressed his hand to the outside of the door then stepped back and waited. Caro knew that he'd wrung a sort of doorbell that would notify the inhabitants that someone was asking to come in. They could then look at the monitor to see who it was.

Seconds later, the door slid up and a gnarled looking male of an undetermined age emerged to greet them.

"Sabin! It is wonderful to see you again, Healer. You're visits are always a time of joy for us." When he turned to look at Caro, the male's mouth fell open and he staggered back a step.

Sabin rushed to support him, leaving Caro afraid to move lest she scare the poor male to death. Why had he looked at her like that?

"Easy, Alsure. This is my and my brother's mate, Caro. She's one of the females from the ship that crashed here several months back."

"A female? Here at our home?" The older male's pale silver skin seemed to grow even lighter. "You remind me of my sister, Kalaih. She had a light hair color, though not nearly as light as yours. I never thought to see a female again."

"Would it be okay for me to visit with you while Sabin is performing his health checks?" Caro asked.

"We would be honored, but we have nothing to greet you with. It wouldn't be right for you to grace us with your beauty and we can't honor you back," the older male said with a sadness in his voice so strong she could almost taste it.

"That is not necessary, Alsure," Sabin began.

"It is, male. That is the way it has always been. Surely, you have not grown lazy with our traditions. Just because our females are no longer with us, we mustn't forget who we were and still are."

"But, sir. You do have something of great value that I would love to share with you," Caro hurried to say.

"What would that be?" He looked completely baffled.

"I was hoping you and your friends would teach me the history and traditions of your people. If I am to live here, I need to know this, and to be honest with you, the learning programs on the information units don't do a good job of explaining it so that it means something to me," she said.

The older male seemed to grow in statue, standing a little straighter than only seconds before. "It would be our honor to teach you about our history and way of life. No one knows it better than those of us who lived it."

"That is what I thought as well. If we are to live here and bear young with your males, we need to know these things to teach our young as they grow. Would others of an age to remember be interested in teaching more of us? There are many of us, and it would really help us to understand why things are as they are." Caro held her breath, waiting as the male seemed to consider her request.

"I'm sure they will all be just as anxious to meet the other females and offer their memories as tribute for the treat of their presence," the older male said. "Please come in. I want to introduce you to my family here."

Caro smiled and reached out for the male's hand. She almost missed the tears in the older male's eyes as he beamed and gently took her much smaller hand. His were gnarled and callused with what she figured were age spots all over the back of it.

Alsure slowly led her into the entrance of the home, and over to the commons area where several other older males in various stages of health sat talking. The room hushed into an expectant silence when one by one the males noticed her presence next to Alsure. A few of the males even allowed their mouths to drop open, flashing various degrees of tooth loss among the aged males.

"Family, this is Caro. She is the mate to Sabin, our healer, and his brother, Gressen. She has come with him today to learn from us about our history," Alsure said.

"A female. Look, Soku, a real female. I barely remember my Cleatha. I miss her still," one of the males with some type of walker said, elbowing the male next to him.

"I've got two eyes, male. I can see." The disgruntled, sour looking Levassian's braid hung over his shoulder, making Caro wonder where it came from since the rest of his head looked like a shiny blue-black bowling ball, devoid of any hair whatsoever.

"Hello," Caro said offering her hand.

Bowling ball's mouth fell open as he took a shaky step back using his odd-looking cane for support.

Caro instantly dropped her hand, looking at Sabin to see if she'd done something wrong. Sabin's amused expression assured her she'd done nothing inappropriate.

"I'm sorry. I didn't mean to upset you." Caro smiled at the male but didn't offer her hand again.

"Do not bother about Soku. He's always sour these days," Alsure told her with a wink.

"Do not speak for me, Alsure. I have a right to my feelings," Soku grumbled.

"Come. You must visit us in the common room," Alsure said, turning to herd the other elders out of the entryway.

Caro counted six males gathered in the large room. It was nearly impossible to guess their ages. She had no idea how they aged on this planet. If she had to guess, they were all between the age of eighty and ninety, but the length of days and years was different on Levasso.

Gressen had explained that they revolved around the two suns a little slower than their Earth, according to the information they'd managed to harvest from the databases that hadn't been destroyed in the crash. They figured that their year lasted four hundred and five days compared to the three hundred sixty-five days of Earth. Each day consisted of thirty hours. In the growing period of their planet, what was considered to be day, lasted fifteen hours, though full light lasted nearly thirteen of those hours.

"What has made you wish to learn from us, female?" one of the other males asked in a broken, raspy voice.

"This is Aveste, Caro. He is one of our honored ones who fought in one of our battles. He was injured but still managed to hold off the enemy until more of us arrived. All of his team had been hurt in a blast and were unable to assist," Sabin told her.

"Hush, young male," the hero fussed. "I am talking to the female, not you. You, we can talk to anytime."

Caro couldn't stop the giggle that erupted at hearing Sabin chastised. Her male ducked his head but a small smile remained on his face.

"Ah, that is music that I hear. The sweetest of melodies we have not heard in so long I had forgotten its sound until now." A much shorter male shuffled forward, a wistful expression tight on his face as he turned his ear toward her.

"The poet is Vesper," Soku bit out in a sour tone.

When Caro looked over at the grumpy elder, one corner of his mouth had lifted into a crooked smile, softening his tone a bit. It was obvious to her, at least, that he liked this Vesper male.

"It's great to meet you, Vesper. Thank you for saying that. I never thought of my laugh as a pleasing sound before." Caro smiled at the male and nodded her head at him.

"Please sit and tell us a bit about you, mate of Gressen and Sabin." Alsure indicated the assortment of chairs placed haphazardly around the room.

On closer examination though, Caro realized it was a path of sorts that gave the males plenty of room to maneuver with their various devices that helped them to walk. One of the males sat on some sort of contraption that scooted him easily around the room without any indication there was a steering wheel or handles. She made a note to ask Sabin about it later.

"Please, everyone, take your favorite seats. I don't want to sit until you are all comfortable," she told them.

The males all stilled as if they'd been flash frozen in place. Their expressions would have been comical if not for the fact that Caro was afraid she'd said something to upset them. She didn't move either, just waited on one of them to stir first. Finally, after what seemed like forever, Soku stomped as much as possible with the stick over to a large oddly shaped chair and eased himself down before propping the cane thing next to him.

"I am too old to stand around waiting for an uneducated female to decide where she wishes to sit." Soku crossed his gnarled hands on his lap and stared hard at Caro. "You're supposed to sit down first, mate of Sabin."

Caro wasn't going to let the grumpy elder intimidate her. She deliberately walked over to Soku's chair and sat on the wide arm of the oddly shaped chair, leaning her back against the protruding side of the chair's back. To her surprise, it was fairly comfortable. She clasped her hands in her lap and crossed one leg before looking at the other males still frozen in place.

"I've chosen my seat. You should all find one now."

Sabin winked at her when she looked over to where he was standing behind one of the males in the wheelchair-like cart. It was all the encouragement she needed to say more.

"In my culture, our elders are treated with respect and awe. It would be rude for anyone to sit before them or to take their seat. We believe that our elders deserve the best of everything for their part in shaping our lives and our country. They were the backs on which the younger generations stood to reach their goals in life. They've earned the right to demand respect and to be grumpy and ornery." Caro made sure to look down at Soku when she said grumpy. The rest of the elders noticed and chuckled in appreciation.

"It is not that way here. We are happy that they remember to see to our food and keep our rooms clean for us. No one comes to visit or check on us other than the healers," Soku grumbled.

"And of the healers, Sabin is the only one who spends more time than it takes to check us and walk out of the door," Aveste added.

"Sabin has explained that with fewer of our males able to work, they must spend more time performing their duties. It leaves little time to spend with us, Soku," Alsure chastised.

"That is an excuse to cover for the younger males' negligence of us." Soku cleared his throat then continued. "The truth of the matter is that with fewer males to feed and provide for, the need for the same amount of food and products is decreased as well. Even with more elders than young, the need is not that great. We eat very little. Our bodies don't require as much since we don't do as much as before. It is only an excuse they choose to hide behind."

Caro felt so bad for the elders. They weren't addle-brained. They might not be physically able to labor with the younger males, but their minds were still sharp and their feelings just as brittle as ever. They deserved so much more and still had a substantial archive of knowledge to contribute to their society.

"Well, I for one recognize the vast resources you represent that is desperately needed. When the young begin to be born here, they will need teachers and examples of integrity and strength to learn from. I would hope you might consider helping to shape their young minds. Before that though, there is a need for our people to learn your history and traditions. We can't become integrated into your society without a great deal of trouble otherwise. Are you willing to teach us?" Caro held her breath, praying they would accept her offer to become part of society once more.

The elder males looked around at each other, their wrinkled faces and aged eyes betraying nothing of their feelings concerning her question. Instead, they began standing up once again, Soku using his stick and the opposite arm to get to his feet. Caro was afraid she'd insulted them or hurt their feelings. She started to stand and apologize for making assumptions, but Sabin shook his head so she remained as she was.

"Precious female called Caro. You alone have seen our plight and that we are not useless despite our physical decline. We would be honored to teach your females and the young of those unions." This came from Aveste in his rough voice made raspier by the obvious emotion displayed on his face.

"With no young since many years ago, there are no education facilities for them when they come of age. I'm sure the council hasn't thought ahead that far, but with the declining work force, that needs to be addressed, sooner rather than later. It will take time to build and supply them," Alsure added with a smile.

Caro slid off the arm of the chair and acted on impulse. To Soku's surprise, as well as every other male in the room's surprise, she kissed the old male's cheek, then proceeded to do the same or give a hug to each of the males in the room.

"Thank you all for agreeing to help us. No one else on Levasso is as knowledgeable of the past and what it has to say about our future as the elders of the planet. I'm going to talk to all of you in the next few days and arrange for the females who are not already doing something else to visit with you all and learn. I'm so excited to be a part of this." Caro couldn't believe that she was going to help make a difference to an entire society. It was a sobering realization.

Caro sat and talked with the elder males as Sabin made his rounds, checking each of them and mending minor problems as he went. By the time they'd finished with the first family home, it was time for lunch. They ate in one of the numerous abandoned homes that were still maintained to a certain degree. Sabin had brought a sandwich of sorts for them and a substance that was a little like their tea back on Earth. Gressen had told her it was made from the root of a plant called a boa plant. It was covered in thorns which protected it from the creatures on the planet so it was nearly impossible to harvest by hand.

"Sweet Caro, you charmed them like I knew you would. More than that, you captured a truth the younger males haven't been able to understand. It is a concept that eludes them to this day. Now they will come to realize how foolish they have been to ignore our greatest strengths and assets." Sabin leaned over and kissed her lightly on the lips. "You truly are a wonder, our very own miracle."

"I'm just me, Sabin. I'm not a miracle. I'm a female who remembers what I learned at my grandparent's feet as a young child. Those were some of my fondest memories, and where I learned the basic principles of life. I remember my papa telling me that if I learned how to listen, forgive, and always smile, I would never lose my way in life. I would always have the keys to finding my way back. And you know what, Sabin? He was right." Caro leaned against her mate, thankful that they were working things out between the three of them.

"The elders are right. You are an amazing female who sees far more than what is in front of you. You are able to see the soul of a male and know his worth. I'm so lucky to have a piece of your heart, sweetness," Sabin said.

Caro knew she was blushing from the heat in her cheeks. At least this time it hadn't spread to her neck, yet. Why was she always doing that around them?

"I'm lucky to have crashed on a planet with two males who care about me for me, and not for what I look like or what I can give them."

"I remember Gressen telling me that once he saw your eyes shining with determination and hope, he wanted to be worthy of you. He wanted to believe in the hope you had and watch what your determination could bring. My brother was right. He always is. Your determination to contribute has opened an entire new life for our elders and set the foundation for our future young. You are truly amazing, Caro." Sabin brushed his lips across hers once more.

Caro wanted more than just a kiss, but knew they still needed to visit several more of the elders that afternoon. Spending time with Sabin or Gressen or both together deserved more than a few stolen minutes. Maybe one day when they were much older and had been together longer, they would be satisfied with stolen moments, but she refused to compromise yet.

"We should go and see the others," she suggested even as she caressed his cheek. "Maybe if we finish early we can convince Gressen to take a nap before last meal."

Sabin's eyes lit up while his mouth curved up into a smile. Caro loved their smiles for more reasons than one. The main one though was that she put them there when before they rarely smiled at all, they always had one for her.

Chapter Twelve

"I'm so glad Heidi is going with me every day. She's quiet, but so patient with the elders," Caro told Gressen and Sabin as they finished up their last meal.

"I'm glad she is, too," Gressen said. "I worry about you by yourself. The other females who are working with the elders work in pairs."

"But it's safe. You've assured me that no one would ever hurt a female. The biggest danger is stumping my toe or banging my finger in the door at the lodge that still sticks," she said giving Gressen an eye.

"I know. They are working on this lodge, as you call it, as much as possible. You really shouldn't go there at all until they have it finished. There are too many things that could happen while they are working, Caro."

Gressen carried the dirty dishes to the automatic washer. "I wasn't sure how this lodge would work, but it is a unique blend of our world and yours."

"I like it as well. It has a lot of safety features that will make it much easier for our elders to get around. The site she chose for it is central to all of their family homes, so no one has more than two lengths to get to it," Sabin said.

"Caro, the transport is going to work well at taking them to and from the new school that is planned, but it would really go a long way to placating Tanus if you would stop calling it the wienermobile. It offends him, Caro." Gressen's smile told her that he felt obligated to remind her of it, but secretly enjoyed the dig she made at the uptight male who always managed to be rude without appearing to be.

The male referred to Caro as Gressen and Sabin's social female. Caro hadn't realized what it meant at first, and neither Sabin nor Gressen had intended for her to ever find out, but Soku outwitted them. He became enraged the first time he heard the snobby male call her that. Now Caro enjoyed calling his prized transport the wienermobile just to upset him. At least it had kept Soku from devising all sorts of ways to get back at him. She really didn't want there to be an all-out war between the two males.

"But it's so perfect, Gressen. I wish you could have seen the commercial back on Earth. You'd understand then. Besides, he called me a social female, and it didn't appear to upset you one bit. He'd basically called me a loose female. Back on earth they were called sluts, and the only person who could call you a slut then was your best friend or your man." She stuck her hands on her hips and did her best to glare at the two stubborn males. It didn't go over as she wanted it to.

Sabin laughed. "He says he's using your terminology to say that you are a social butterfly, which your informational data says is someone who likes to interact with other people and exchange information."

"We aren't exactly sure how talking about clothes is exchanging information, but some of your traditions are odd to us anyway," Gressen said.

"Oh, you males! Fine. Don't lecture me about the wienermobile, and I won't fuss about his insult." Caro loved trading jabs like this. She'd never had a close friend or lover she could do this with and feel comfortable enough with their loyalty that they wouldn't use it against her someday.

Everything about her new life was working out perfectly. She'd had a slow start and with all of the misunderstandings it was a wonder the three of them had managed to get things right, but she didn't regret one thing. She was sure the reason Della and her mates had made it work so quickly was that one of them was also human. Kane had compromised a lot at first to make things work between them. Most men, males, weren't able to do that. It offended their pride and ego to allow another male to take the lead in anything.

"How are you feeling, sweetness?" Sabin asked, pulling her carefully into his arms.

"I'm fine, Sabin. Why?"

"You appeared a little tired and pale when you returned from your visit with the elders in the eastern home. That is a long way to go after you've already been to the southern border. Maybe you should limit your visits to one home a day. You've got many of the other females helping now." Sabin's eyes narrowed even as she shook her head.

"I love going to see them. It isn't too much. Goodness, when I was working back on Earth, I would sometimes fly across the country twice in one day. It doesn't even take an hour to go from the eastern to the western parts of Levastah." Caro stuck her tongue out at him.

"Sabin's right, Caro. You keep forgetting that our atmosphere and suns drain you of energy much faster than your one sun and lighter air ratios. We are not sure if you will ever adjust to this or not, but we have hopes that it will at least improve over time." Gressen ran his hand down her hair, tugging at the ends before closing the heating element and washer.

"But I don't feel any different. I'm sure you're just seeing things, Sabin. You check me all the time. One would think you were trying to play doctor with me or something," Caro teased.

"Play doctor? Doctor is your healer back on Earth, right? Why would I want to play doctor when I *am* a healer?" Sabin's puzzled expression was so cute that Caro burst into laughter.

"We've got to improve your sex knowledge, Sabin." She turned to Gressen and grabbed his hand. "Yours, too, warrior male."

"I do not think we need education on sexual relations, Caro." Gressen appeared so indignant that she giggled.

"No. Not in that sense, but you don't know anything about messing around. There is a difference between making love, having sex, and messing around. Oh, and there's also just plain old fucking as well." She loved seeing their eyes darken when she started talking dirty to them.

The two males had talked enough to Kane and the other human males to know some of the basics of each of those terms, but not enough to truly understand the differences. Caro wanted to show them everything, over and over and over again.

* * * *

The moment Caro stepped into their room, Gressen was on her. He pulled her into his arms, still managing to be careful with her despite his enormous strength and size. She loved how he kissed, intense and demanding, so unlike Sabin who took tender to an entirely new level. She enjoyed Sabin's kisses just as much as his brother's, but there were times when it was Gressen's aggressive mouth she needed.

"Step back, brother. I can't remove her robes with you pressed against her like that." Sabin's voice held a note of need in it that Caro hadn't remembered hearing before.

"Easy, Sabin." Gressen eased back without releasing her.

As soon as Sabin had her robes removed, Gressen resumed kissing her senseless. The way he devoured her, running his tongue across all the sensitive areas in her mouth, made her knees weak. His tongue tangled with hers then massaged it so that she felt it all over her body. When he finally pulled back, Caro wondered if she'd be able to stand if he suddenly let go.

She needn't have worried because Sabin was right there to take over. The male turned her to face him as Gressen began to undress. Sabin nipped her chin then licked it with a growl that turned her on. She'd never heard him make that noise before. He slowly and methodically kissed and licked his way around her jaw, behind her ear, down her neck, to torment her collarbone. Nothing about his seduction was hurried, despite his earlier desperation to rid her of her robes.

"Need you so much," he said in a hoarse whisper.

"I need you, too."

"Ease her to the bed, brother," Gressen whispered behind her.

Caro felt her world tilt as they settled her back on the bed and dove in after her. The males quickly gravitated to their favorite areas, proving that all males, no matter what race or species, had favorite female body parts. For Sabin, it was her breasts. He seemed fascinated by the way he could squeeze and move them around. He liked seeing his fingerprints there, and would gently squeeze with all five fingers, then quickly pull back to watch them form then slowly fade.

He always went to sleep with at least one hand on one of her boobs, and if she woke before they did, he still had one in his hand. It wasn't until the third or fourth night that they shared a bed together that he explained that, though he'd never seen a Levassian female nude in person, they had healer data reels which taught about every aspect of the male and female Levassian's body. Their females' nipples were very small compared to hers.

Caro explained that hers were thicker and longer than the majority of the Earth's female population, but that all human females had them. She didn't go into any of the deviations that nature threw their way like inverted nipples. He was satisfied that he wasn't hurting her when he explored them, sucking, nipping, and pulling on them until she thought he'd eventually grow tired. It hadn't happened yet.

Gressen, on the other hand, was an ass man. He loved licking and eating her pussy, but he really loved squeezing and slapping at her ass cheeks. Anal sex had become a favorite of his as well. Since they were so careful and enjoyed extended foreplay, Caro was fine with both of them at the same time, or even just one of them in her ass. She never would have believed it if someone had told her she'd come to enjoy it back on Earth. Yet here she was, looking forward to Gressen filling her with his thick, hard dick.

One reason she thought the male enjoyed anal sex was because he felt in control in that position. He was on top of both her and his brother. Plus, she was in a vulnerable position to his one of dominance. Caro would never say anything about it to him since he wouldn't understand that she was fine with it. He'd pull back thinking that she was upset over it.

With all of their differences, she'd come to realize that both males tended to err on the side of caution and over compensate for anything they thought might upset her or hurt her feelings. They really did want only to make her happy. Despite everything, Caro still had trouble believing it, and would find herself holding her breath, waiting for the other shoe to drop. So far, it hadn't happened.

Sabin raked his teeth lightly over her engorged nipples, making her cry out in surprise as hot pleasure filled her body. She felt his light bites all the way to her clit. It began to throb in time with the slight sting in her nipples. It was all Caro could do not to thrust her chest into Sabin's smiling face. He teased her by swiping the tip of his tongue over each nipple only once before ignoring them so he could focus on her neck and collarbone. Caro wanted to scream at him to suck them, suck them hard, but she bit her lower lip to keep from begging.

"Our sweet Caro is hurting for something, brother. What do you think she needs?" Gressen asked in his deep husky voice.

"Maybe she needs a spanking, brother," the quieter of the two brothers said.

Gressen chuckled as Caro gasped. "She didn't expect that to come out of your mouth any more than I did, Sabin. Have you been talking to Kane again?"

"Not this time. I've discovered the human male enjoys telling me things that he knows will fire back at me." Sabin frowned up at his brother before turning back to her. "It is most disturbing that he enjoys this."

"Um, Sabin, its 'back fire' on you, not fire back on you." She struggled not to burst out laughing over the fumbled expression. "It's just a saying people use when something doesn't work quite the way they expected it to."

"Yes, that is what happens. You never react like I believe you are supposed to when I listen to his suggestions. I've resolved to research using the information databases that survived the crash instead," Sabin told her.

"So what made you decide I might need a spanking?" Caro asked using a pouty tone and looking up at the male from beneath her lashes.

"You argued with me when I felt that your health was in question. That is a reason for a spanking. I believe it is called discipline on Earth," he said, nodding as if to reassure himself.

"Sabin, I don't want to do that, brother. I won't hit her to punish her." Gressen had scooted off the foot of the bed but had one knee on top of the mattress.

"I don't think he's looking at that sort of discipline, Gressen. I think he's been looking at what is known on Earth as Dominance and submissive play. It's a type of sexual experience or way of life for some, but most people just use it occasionally to spice up their sex life from time to time." Caro still couldn't believe she was teaching a class on everything to do with sex that doesn't come out of a text manual to a pair of alien males.

Except that, I'm the actual alien, not them. They're supposed to be here on Levasso. I'm supposed to be on Earth.

She sighed, but didn't close her eyes and shake her head as she wanted to. Sarcasm, and just about any other emotion or gesture she could lay claim to, wasn't going to go over well with them. They hadn't had much leeway in their emotional arc in forever. Definitely not since before their ship had crash-landed on the planet. Now the

Levassians were forced to deal with a bunch of hormonal females who'd been jacked up on fertility meds during their trip across the galaxy to an entirely new part of the universe to go cold turkey among a group of essentially celibate males in a world without females. Yep, that about summed it all up.

It was the only reason she thought they were letting her do it. They hungered for the information and experience so they didn't mind that it was coming from her, a female. She knew they were overly protective and caring for the opposite sex, but men, males, didn't normally allow a female to take the lead when it came to sex.

Caro started to tell them that she didn't mind a light spanking, but wasn't into the whole submissive-bondage thing. She never made it past the thought because both brothers covered her nipples with their mouths and sucked long and hard. Her eyes rolled back in her head as they proceeded to blow her mind.

"Oh, God! Yes. Please don't stop." Caro squirmed between them as they each wrapped one hand around the breast they were pleasuring and squeezed while both of them reached down between her legs to slip a finger inside her pussy.

Gressen let go of her nipple with a pop and licked his lips. "She's wet and hot, brother. I feel she's ready for more."

"Yes, please give me more, Gressen."

Sabin chuckled. "Indeed she believes she is, but I think maybe she needs something different this time. I would like for her to suck my cock while you fill her hungry cunt with your dick."

"Someone really has been watching educational porn," Caro gasped out. Their fingers were doing deliciously wonderful things to her, making it hard as hell to think straight.

Who would have known that having two fingers from different men moving in their own ways could be so devastating? Every once in a while, one of them would brush a thumb over her clit, causing her vagina muscles to clench, deepening the pleasure of the two thick fingers inside of her.

"Educational porn." Gressen's brows pulled together as he tried to figure out what she meant.

"Stop analyzing everything. Fuck me, Gressen. I want to suck your brother's cock while you pound into me with that great big thick dick." Caro pulled out every dirty word she could think of right then and began teaching them what it was like just to screw for the pleasure of it.

"Turn her over," Sabin said. "She will be better able to take me into her mouth on her hands and knees."

Gressen helped her rearrange herself so that she would be comfortable taking both of them. Sabin positioned himself in front of her on his knees with his back leaning against the headboard while his brother knelt behind her, squeezed, and rubbed her ass cheeks. She could feel the heat from his body warm the backs of her thighs.

Caro looked up at Sabin as he looked down at her. She licked her lips in a slow sensual move before leaning forward to run her tongue over the crown of his cock. He dropped his head back so that it hit the headboard with a thump. She watched as he tightened his grip at the base of his shaft and gritted his teeth. It turned her own even more to know that she could affect him that way.

While she was admiring the bounty before her, Gressen had started pressing his thick dick against her slit. The pressure as he slowly entered her took her breath. It felt so good, so very good. She had to think how to breathe for a second then turned her attention back to Sabin and the equally impressive prick waiting for her.

Caro dragged her tongue from his balls all the way up his shaft before curling it under the mushroomed crown. His swift indrawn breath let her know he was enjoying himself. It was all she needed to know as she slid the tip of it back and forth over the slit at the top.

"Hmmm, you taste so good. Are you going to give me a taste to tide me over until you come for me?" she asked in her most sultry voice possible.

"Caro. Sweet, Caro," Sabin breathed out.

She smiled and sucked his cockhead in, applying as much suction as she could until she heard him growl and his long fingers thread their way through her hair to her scalp. Then she took more of him, inch by slow inch, until she'd taken all she could even with her throat relaxed. He and his brother put even the well-endowed men of earth to shame. She was proud she could even wrap her mouth around his thick dick in the first place.

When she slowly pulled back up until just the crown remained in her mouth, Caro hummed as she slid back down the shaft. She would have smiled at the strangled noise that slipped from between Sabin's lips if there had been any room for her mouth to move.

"Sabin, brother. You look as if she is torturing you. Does it really hurt?" Gressen asked as he pressed deeper into her pussy.

It took a few seconds for him to respond, and then his answer seemed squeezed out of his mouth. "Yes, no. She's torturing me, but it feels so amazing. It almost hurts, but it doesn't."

Gressen chuckled. "You seem confused. Are you sure you're okay?"

"I understand why the males of her race often seem confused when we talk with them. They have been starved of oxygen too many times when they have sex," Sabin said in a quick pant. "I think I will end up suffering the same affliction happily."

"I'll help you with your trouble, Sabin." Gressen's tone should have prepared her for something, but Caro was concentrating too hard on making Sabin feel good.

Gressen pulled back from her pussy, but this time when he slid back in again, he didn't press slowly inside as before. Instead, he powered into her. Caro gasped and an inch more of Sabin's massive dick slid deeper into her throat. She swallowed convulsively around him even as she pulled back.

"Aggaaaa," Gressen's strangled yell as he pulled back out and pistoned in again had Caro struggling to time her oral ministrations on Sabin's shaft so that he didn't cause her to choke.

The faster he thrust, the harder Caro sucked. The quick brushes of his swollen cockhead over her tender tissues elicited unfathomable pleasure inside her cunt. The only way it could have possibly been any better was if they were both pumping their dicks inside of her at the same time with one in her pussy and one in her ass. But, Caro wasn't complaining one bit. She loved the heady feeling of giving Sabin this kind of pleasure, knowing he was beyond control as he dug his nails into her scalp. She knew that if he were in any form of control or knew what he was doing, he would have been horrified at the thought of harming her. Even if she told him how good it felt and that it added to her pleasure.

"So hot and wet. Suns, she's perfect, brother." Gressen continued to tunnel in and out of her pussy, his strokes becoming more frantic and less coordinated the closer he came to release.

"Caro, let go, sweetness. I don't want to choke you," Sabin yelled out. "Please precious one."

She knew their orgasms were much harder than the human males were, but she didn't want to lose that connection to him. She tucked her tongue up against the roof of her mouth to create a small barrier in front of her throat and rubbed the tip of his penis against the ribbed upper pallet of her mouth. He groaned then shouted as he shot loads of thick cum until it overflowed and dripped out of the corners of her mouth.

"Caro, Suns, Caro. Are you okay?" Sabin jerked his dick from her mouth and immediately dropped to the bed so he could look up at her. "Please tell me you are okay."

She swallowed hard while nodding her head. She hadn't expected there to be quite this much, but she could handle it. The way he'd yelled as he came told her how much he'd enjoyed it. She would endure anything to see the painful pleasure painted across his face.

"I'm fine, Sabin. Ohhhhh!" She lost her breath as Gressen returned to fucking her with a purpose.

"Her pleasure point, Sabin. Rub her clit before I lose control. I want her to climax before me." Gressen's voice had dipped to a growly octave that sent chills down Caro's spine.

She arched her back, giving Gressen more of her to hold on to, and Sabin more room to reach beneath her to finger her clit. Stars exploded behind her eyelids as she squeezed them shut with the force of the orgasm they squeezed from her. Her ass and thighs contracted over and over again with the waves of pleasure until she began to cramp.

Gressen seemed to understand because he started squeezing her ass as he rutted against her until, with a loud shout, he ejaculated deep inside of her, the force and heat of his semen almost bruising with intensity. The stimulation had Caro moaning with aftershocks of her own release.

The three of them collapsed in a pile so that all that was heard were the desperate gasps for oxygen and the occasional groan as a new muscle that had worked too hard made itself known.

"I need a shower. I'm sticky all over," Caro finally managed to get out.

"Don't care. You're not moving. We'll clean up in the morning," Gressen fussed in a whiney tone.

Caro knew then that she was in love. Even when they'd left Earth with their sole reason for being allowed the chance at continuing to live was to birth the future generation of humans on some remote planet, she'd never once thought about love or the possibility of falling in love with either or both of her husbands. It hadn't seemed possible as cold and hardened as her heart had become over the years working in the modeling industry. How had they managed to thaw her prison so fast? How had years of built up resentment and hurt just melted away with nothing more than honest kindness?

She relaxed between the two males who were fast becoming her entire world and let it all go. It didn't matter in the end. All that mattered was how they felt about her and their future together. She wanted to ask them, but knew she'd never be satisfied unless they told her on their own terms.

I really do love them. I never believed love would find me, and here I am, millions of miles away from Earth, and it found me anyway.

She whispered, "I love you" to the darkened room filled with low snores. Hopefully, one day soon, she'd hear them back.

Chapter Thirteen

"Thanks for coming with me, Heidi. How are you getting along with Fellen?" Caro asked the shy green-eyed woman as they walked the last half mile to the eastern home.

"He's very good to me. He makes me smile and laugh. No one has ever treated me like that before." Her eyes widened and a frown took over. "I don't mean the other males didn't treat me well, but they seemed so, I don't know, stiff."

"I think a lot of the males here don't know how to express emotions, Heidi. They haven't had women or females to elicit any sort of emotion in them. We're emotional, and we tend to go through life bleeding that off on everyone around us. I honestly think males absorb our emotions and feelings and make them their own." Caro had thought a lot about that over the last few days. She could easily see a change in how her males reacted about things now.

"Well, Fellen has loosened up a lot. He tells me sweet things all the time. I tell him that he should write them down and make a book of poetry, but he doesn't understand the idea. He said why write them down since no one would ever read them, and that reading them would be the only way to feel their meaning." Heidi shrugged. "I didn't know what to say to that."

"Don't push it. I think we are making changes in the Levassians a little at a time. I just hope we aren't changing things too much so that they become us back on Earth. I think a lot of how they live and all is great, peaceful," Caro said.

"Maybe we can help them learn the best parts of our culture without the worst parts." Heidi smiled then ducked her head.

"Maybe," Caro agreed.

They'd just reached the entrance to the elder's house when Caro began to feel dizzy and weak. Heidi saw something in her face and grabbed her arms to steady her.

"Caro! Are you okay?"

"I—I'm just a little tired. The guys think I'm trying to do too much. Maybe they're right. I'll rest once we're inside."

Heidi didn't look convinced, but when Caro walked over to the door to press her hand on the pad next to the door, she didn't say anything more. The dizziness faded, but she was still tired and out of breath. The door opened and Soku appeared. He had his usual scowl in place but it melted away when he saw them standing in the doorway.

"Are you okay, female?" he asked stepping back to hold the door open wider. "You look pale."

Before she could say anything, Alsure shuffled into the entrance and stared at her. "Soku is right. Come in and rest. It is always good to see you and your friends, but maybe you should rest more and visit less. Aren't your males watching over you?"

"Alsure, I'm fine. They take good care of me. I think I forget that your two suns tend to drain a human if we're out in it too much. How is everyone doing today?" She turned the conversation away from how she felt. She didn't want them worrying about her.

I don't understand. I've never felt this way before. Two weeks ago, a week ago, I made these trips without even noticing it. Maybe Sabin should check me out when I return home.

"Hello, Aveste. How are you doing this day?" Caro asked when they'd entered the common room.

"I am fine, female. We just finished the noon meal. If you haven't eaten, we can make you plates with ease," Aveste said.

Today, his silver colored hair lay over one shoulder, but as normal for him, he didn't braid it. Caro couldn't help but wonder why, but wasn't going to be nosey and ask. She knew his raspy voice was from a war injury, but not much else about him or the other males.

"Thank you, but we ate before we started out," Heidi told them.

She was so much more animated and open around the elder males than she was around anyone else, unless it was her Fellen. She wasn't sure what it was about them that allowed her to relax and be herself. Caro was just glad that she had this outlet. She was a beautiful girl in her sweetness and the way she treated everyone around her. On Earth, she was probably ignored or worse, teased, but here, she was accepted and it was obvious that Fellen adored her.

She and Heidi visited with the elders who sat in the common room, though Heidi carried the conversation, seeming to realize that Caro didn't feel herself. The elders talked about the theories concerning the great Eros scourge that had all but wiped out their females. Some believed it had been sent to them by their enemies. Others felt it was a result of their deity finding fault with them.

"Who is your deity, Soku," Caro asked. "I've never really heard anything about the Levassians having one."

"Deity is the all-knowing one who created all of the universes and filled them with planets and moons and creatures to entertain himself. Most of us have forgotten Deity, believing he moved on to some other place to create and has forgotten his first made." Soku shook his head, a sad defeated expression that she hadn't seen since the first day they'd met seemed to take root on his face. Caro didn't like seeing that on him.

"Maybe when everyone blamed the Eros scourge on Deity, it hurt him, and he's just waiting on you to say you're sorry and respect him again," she suggested.

Soku nodded but didn't reply. Alsure and Aveste both nodded but didn't say anything either. It was Heidi who changed the subject and started them all talking again. Caro listened but didn't contribute much. She still had the oddest feeling of not quite dizzy and not quite nauseas, but somewhere in between. And she was so tired.

"Caro, have there been any more matings with the females?" Aveste asked.

"What? Um, no. Not that I've been told." She smiled at Heidi. "I have high hopes with this one though."

Heidi blushed and ducked her head. "We don't know each other very well yet, Caro."

The elders all laughed with Alsure patting her hand. "Give it time, young female. Take the time you need to feel comfortable before you make any decisions."

"Yes, they've waited many years for the chance to find a female," Aveste said. "A few more weeks won't hurt them."

"Weeks?" Heidi squeaked out.

Soku frowned and glared over at Aveste. "Scare her to death why don't you."

Caro suppressed a smile to see the normally crotchety elder defend poor Heidi. The young female had a way of eliciting those feelings toward her.

"Don't worry, Heidi. You have all the time in the world to decide how to spend the rest of your life. It isn't like on Earth where you either date for months or grow up with someone you eventually marry. We don't know these males, and have to become comfortable around them and be able to trust them with our hearts. Take your time." Caro sighed. "We probably should head back now."

"You're right. If we're late, the males get upset," Heidi agreed.

"They worry about you, female. It is hard to allow you to wander around on your own. For so many years, we've taught them that females are to be hidden away and protected with everything they have," Alsure told them. "Cater to them and give them no reason to worry. It will go a long way in helping your females to make slow changes that are good and safe."

"You're wise as always, Alsure. Thank you." Caro slowly stood up, keeping one hand on the arm of the seat as she did.

"We have greatly enjoyed your visit. The other males will be back again to help in the education the next time you are able to come. We were most happy that one of the males thought to take them to visit some of the other elders. You've made many positive changes in our way of life, Caro. Thank you," Aveste said.

"It isn't just me. Della has had a much greater influence than I have with her nearly daily talks with your council. I'm just grateful you have agreed to help us learn about our new home and the traditions you hold as important." Caro placed a hand on Heidi's arm to urge her toward the door.

"May you be healthy and happy in the coming days, Caro. Heidi, be healthy and happy," Soku told them as the others murmured their traditional good-byes along with him.

She and Heidi returned the sentiments then walked through the door into the still bright sunlight. Almost immediately, Caro felt the weight of the dual suns on her strength. She'd always noticed the difference between Levasso and Earth, but it seemed that instead of growing more accustomed to those differences, she was succumbing to them.

I need to listen to the guys more. They have lived here all their lives and I'm new. I think I'll take the day off tomorrow and rest at home. If I make it back, that is. I'm so darn tired.

Caro stumbled and was grateful when Heidi caught her. The young female looked at her with obvious worry bright in her eyes. She didn't say anything, but remained close as they continued walking back to their homes.

Less than halfway there, Caro became so dizzy and weak that she couldn't take another step. Before she could even warn Heidi, the bright sunshine that was nearly blinding at times dimmed until there was nothing and Caro collapsed.

* * * *

Sabin's heart was in his throat as he and Gressen rushed to get Caro. They were using one of the clinic's transports so they could get her back as fast as possible. Heidi had run back to the elder's home and had them call for help while she'd gone back to sit with Caro. He would be sure she and her protector knew how grateful they were.

"What could be wrong, brother? She seemed fine when she left this morning." Gressen drummed his fingers on his thigh as Sabin operated the controls in order to get them there as fast as possible.

"I don't know. We will find out. She's been much more tired than usual these last few days. Nothing showed up on the scans, but I only did cursory ones to pick up any normal illness. I won't make that mistake again, no matter how much she complains." He couldn't stop worrying that he'd made a serious, maybe even life-threatening mistake with the female that had become his world. How was he supposed to balance keeping her happy and keeping her safe and healthy?

"She will be fine, Sabin. None of the other females have had any serious illnesses, so it can't be something that is caused by our planet and the differences in atmosphere, or more would be ill by now," he said.

"There they are, just ahead. The elders are all with them." Sabin was so grateful that they had erected a shelter over the two females. It looked like they had enlisted aid from some younger males to hold the shelter in place.

As soon as he'd secured the transport, both of them jumped from the control cab and hurried over to where Caro lay with her head on Heidi's lap. On one side stood a very old saufass tree with some of its fruit still hanging from the low hanging branches. On the other side, the elders and younger males stood blocking the suns.

"Thank you all for your help with our mate," Gressen said.

"I'm so glad you're here," Heidi said. "I've been worried. She hasn't woken up."

"Did she hit her head when she collapsed," Sabin asked her as he ran a quick scan to assure that there were no broken bones or concussion.

"No. I caught her as she fell and eased her to the ground. I didn't know whether to stay with her and hope someone came by, or to find help. I hope I did the right thing," Heidi said, choking back a sob.

"You did everything just right, female. Do not berate yourself, child," Soku told her.

Sabin couldn't believe the elder male was being so gentle with the young female when he'd been nothing but foul and bitter with anyone who made the mistake of crossing his path for as long as he'd know the male. He put that to the back of his mind as he concentrated on his mate.

"Sabin?" Gressen asked as he hovered next to him, obviously afraid to touch her.

"I don't see anything wrong at first glance. Her temperature is a little higher than normal, but that is to be expected since she's been outside. I believe it is safe to move her, and I can do a full scan and diagnostic back at the clinic. Let's load her into the transport." Sabin packed away his instruments before turning to Heidi. "Has she said anything about feeling bad over the last few days?"

"She hasn't said anything at all about that, but I've noticed that she seemed a little less energetic of late, and she didn't interact with all of us as much. It was almost as if she were distracted by something that worried her," Heidi said.

"Is she going to be okay, Sabin? Is there anything we can do to help?" Aveste rasped out.

"She will be fine. I will make sure of it. You have all been more than impressive with caring for her. Gressen and I are in your debt for your assistance," Sabin said.

"Olfre, Casden. Make sure the elders return home safely," Gressen ordered. "Heidi, you will ride with us. I'll call your male to pick you up at the clinic."

"Th—thank you. Are you sure I won't be in the way?" she asked.

"No, you will be fine, and may be able to help me keep her comfortable during the ride," Sabin told her.

He nodded at the group of males watching them, then helped Gressen gently transfer her to the hover board before guiding it to the back of the transport where his brother had thought ahead to leave the back open. They quickly loaded her and secured the board to the floor for safety. Gressen helped Heidi up into the back where she took the seat he pointed out to her and strapped in.

"Ready back there?" Gressen asked once he'd climbed back into the control cabin.

"Ready. Let's get her to the clinic, brother."

The commute back to the clinic seemed to take forever, but Sabin knew it was much faster than the one to where Caro had been lying unconscious had been. Gressen was a more aggressive driver when operating a transport than Sabin tended to be. But Sabin didn't drive that often since they normally had a clinician assistant drive to and from picking someone up in need of care.

"Heidi, use that cloth next to you to lay across her forehead. It is a temperature regulator and will cool her off some." He watched as the female took the specially designed cloth and carefully laid it over Caro's forehead, then looked up to make sure she'd done it right.

Sabin nodded and continued to monitor her vital signs with his handheld unit. So far, they all looked within normal limits according to the information they'd gleamed from the spacecraft's databases. When he looked up, a sign advising that the clinic was just ahead flashed by. Sabin let out a sigh of relief. The sooner they got her inside and under the full-body diagnostic scanners, the better he would feel.

"The assistants are about to open the back to unload her, Sabin. I'm going to call Fellen for Heidi. I'll be in after that." Gressen disappeared from the control cab just as the transport's back door engaged to open.

Sabin spent the next five minutes directing the assistants on what to do and transferring Caro to the full-body scanner. One of the techs took blood samples before rushing away to run the samples through their array of tests.

Once his mate was settled in the scanner, Sabin brushed the back of his fingers across her cheek, then stepped back to close the system. It didn't completely enclose her in a tube, but only a hand's breath separated the top from the bottom all the way around.

Sabin took the controls and began setting up the various scans to run, praying he would be able to figure out the cause of her collapse and earlier weakness. So far, nothing had shown up on the initial scans, but there were many more to cycle through. Then there was the blood sample results that might shine some light on the issue.

"How is she?" Gressen asked, stepping into the secluded room.

"The same. Nothing has shown up yet. Did you reach Fellen for Heidi?"

"He is on his way to retrieve her now. He thanked us for caring for her despite our own mate's illness. He wished her well and said as soon as we know anything to please let his Heidi know. Fellen was positive she would be very worried and anxious to know about her friend." Gressen reached his hand toward the opening of the scanner, but quickly withdrew it, knowing that all it would do was burn him as well as disrupt the scan.

"Patience, brother. We'll know something soon. So far, nothing has become apparent. I'll let you know once something does." Sabin didn't take his eyes off of the controls.

"I'll be right here until you know something," Gressen said.

"Hopefully we won't have to wait for long. I want to start treatment as soon as possible."

"Healer, Sabin. I have some results for you to view," one of the assistants said as he held out a display unit.

"Excellent, thank you." Sabin scrolled through the results pleased that at first glance, nothing seemed all that out of place. Then he noticed that her iron was low as well as her sodium and potassium."

"What is it, Sabin?" Gressen asked walking over to him.

"Nothing much except that she has low iron which is what helps with making red blood cells that carry oxygen around the body. Low iron will make her weak, tired, and dizzy. Over time it can cause heart problems as well." Sabin easily repeated his knowledge to his brother.

"What do we do to correct it?" Gressen asked.

"Make sure she consumes enough in the future. She could have trouble absorbing it from the food she is eating, but none of the other females seem to be affected yet."

"There has to be more to this illness than just some low iron." Gressen paced the length of the room and back.

"She also has some low electrolytes, which I would expect with the exposure to our two suns. We will correct that deficiency as well. The idea of refusing to let her continue to visit the males doesn't sit well with me. She will be most insistent on continuing anyway."

Gressen rubbed his face with both hands. "You're right, but we can possibly make it so that she has more to do around our home."

"Like what?" Sabin couldn't help but feel it was wrong to trick their mate into working more around home when she preferred to visit with the elders.

"I don't know. I just don't want her to become ill from doing too much. How much longer until you know what is wrong?" Garret began pacing again.

The scanner paused, then started again only to stop and turn off. Sabin had never seen it do that before. He checked the readings, then ran a diagnostic to determine what had stopped it. Nothing showed up. He looked over the last readings, confused at the results. The scanner was obviously malfunctioning. Why now with their mate's health at stake? He'd have to move her to the next room where another scanner was located.

"What's wrong?" Gressen stopped pacing and joined Sabin in front of the control panel. "Did you find what's wrong? Is it bad?"

"Calm down, brother. The scanner appears to have shut down. We will need to move her to the one next door to finish the scan. The results from this one can't be trusted and they don't make sense as it is."

"Why? What do they indicate is wrong?"

"I'm not even sure. It shows two circulatory rhythms with differing speeds and pressures. It doesn't make sense. Hold on while I call an assistant to help move her."

Just as he placed his hand over the pad next to the doorway, it opened and the technician from the path control entered, his eyes so wide Sabin felt his heart stop for several seconds before surging to his throat where it nearly choked him.

"What is it?" he demanded.

Sabin felt Gressen at his back as the obviously worried, or was it shocked, technician held out the results pad with a shaking hand. As soon as Sabin took it, the poor male stepped back to lean against the wall.

It took two tries for him to operate the results pad, then he had to read it three times. He still couldn't believe what he was reading. He slammed the pad into his brother's hands and strode back to the scanner to review the results once more.

They are right. The lab results confirm it. I can't believe it. It just doesn't seem possible that this would happen with all of the blessings they'd had when the females had arrived.

"Sabin! Talk to me. What is wrong?" Gressen's face had paled to a dull bronze, no longer shiny and healthy looking.

"She's with young, brother. We are going to be fathers!"

Chapter Fourteen

Warmth spread through her body, followed by a coolness that settled her stomach and the pounding in her head. What had happened to her? Why couldn't she open her eyes?

I remember visiting the elders with Heidi. I wasn't feeling well when we left. Did I pass out and fall? Was Heidi all right? Where were Gressen and Sabin? They'd take care of her. She knew they would.

"Caro? Can you hear me, sweetness? Wake up for us. We need to see your pretty blue eyes."

She could hear Sabin's voice so far away at first, but it grew closer the more he talked.

"Gressen and I want to talk to you, Caro. Wake up for us."

Caro could hear worry in his voice and tried to tell him not to worry so much, she was just fine. Her voice didn't want to cooperate though. Instead, she worked on opening her eyes and finally managed to pop one lid open before having to squint from the overhead light.

"Turn that light off!"

Gressen's irritated demand amused her. Caro started to laugh but ended up coughing instead.

"Easy, Caro," Sabin told her. Then a straw touched her lips. "Drink a little of this to wet your throat. Just a little, precious."

She sipped from the straw then allowed her body to relax against the comfortable mattress. When she opened her eyes this time, the bright light had been moved and both eyes managed to remain open to take in two very worn and worried males.

"There you are. How are you feeling, Caro?" Sabin asked.

"Like a shirt that's been washed and hung out to dry," she croaked out.

The two males looked at each other with puzzled expression drawing their brows together. She nearly laughed at the sight they made.

"I'm okay, guys. I just meant that I'm exhausted and I don't know why. I feel like I've been scrubbing floors, or maybe washing a car, um, one of those transports. My arms and legs feel weighted down," she finally told them.

"You will need to rest more now, Caro. The exhaustion will improve, but only if you get enough rest in the future. We will need to make some changes to your diet as well." Sabin's words didn't quite make sense to her.

"Maybe I've pushed it a little too much, but I'm fine." She didn't want them to stop her visits with the elders. She loved them and they had progressed so much by having visitors and a purpose once again.

"You will have to take better care of yourself and get more rest like Sabin has told you, Caro." Gressen took one of her hands and squeezed it carefully. "You have so much to get used to, and now there will be even more challenges for us."

Caro narrowed her eyes. "What are you talking about? What challenges?"

Sabin leaned down and kissed her forehead before standing up again. A mixture of emotions clouded his eyes as he seemed to be trying to get his thoughts together. He looked excited, worried, afraid, and happy all at one time. It seemed impossible that all of those expressions could rotate across someone's face like that, but they did.

"Sweet Caro, you are with young," he said.

"Huh?" She wasn't sure what he meant. With young?

That's what the elders call Heidi and I, young females.

"There is a new life growing inside of you, precious," Sabin tried again.

Finally, it sank in and Caro's mouth dropped open. A baby? She was pregnant? The knowledge brought tears to her eyes. She was going to have a baby. No matter how much she'd anticipated becoming a mother, Caro hadn't really thought it all through. It had never seemed real when she'd boarded the ship that would take them to a new home. Now she was broadsided with the news and an all-new worry began to take root in her belly.

"What if I don't make a good mother?" she blurted out along with the tears.

The two males exchanged panicked looks as she burst out crying. How could she explain it to them? They'd never really been around females before and had no clue what to expect with one who was pregnant for the first time in her life. She needed her momma, but Della would do.

"I want Della," she cried. "Please get Della for me."

To her surprise, both of her mates left the room, running into each other at the door as they tried to get through it. If anyone had peeked in right then, they would have been convinced she was insane because she burst out laughing even as she cried at the sight they made trying to put distance between themselves and their overly emotional female.

Ten minutes later, Della burst into the room but there was no sign of her two males.

"I can't believe it! You're going to have a baby!" Della's screech almost hurt her ears.

"I can't believe it either. Did Gressen and Sabin even come back to the clinic with you?" she asked with a grin.

"Yeah, but they made Kane and Veran come with them. What did you do to them?" Della asked, sitting on the side of the bed next to her.

"I started crying," she admitted, a little embarrassed.

"And they haven't been around a female since they were kids. No wonder they looked like they were about to throw up." Della laughed so hard she had to wipe her eyes and hold her stomach.

"Oh, Della. What if I'm a terrible mom? There's no one here to help us get it right," she whined.

"We have each other, honey. It will be fine. You're going to make an excellent mom. And I'm going to be the best aunty ever!"

"Aunty? You better hurry up and have someone for mine to play with. I don't want my kid to grow up without friends. Start working on it!"

Della grinned. "Don't worry, girlfriend. We've been practicing hard for weeks and weeks now."

"Well, stop with the practicing and get down to business. I mean it." It hit her all over again and she burst into tears. "I want to keep visiting with the elders. I don't want them to stop me from doing that, Della."

"They won't, honey. Once you've caught back up with your rest and are eating right, I'm sure they'll let you go, but you're going to have to back off some. This heat and the effects of two suns are just harder than it was on Earth. You have to accept that and get more rest." Della squeezed her hands with a smile.

Caro knew she was right but it didn't make her feel much better. Suddenly she was tired again. She yawned and had to fight to open her eyes again afterward.

"You need to take a nap, Caro. Rest. You're going to be so busy for the next six or seven months you won't be able to keep up. Every female and male in the city is going to want to wish you well. This is a huge event for them. A child. A real, newborn infant that will grow up in front of them is about to be born!"

"I could have done without you reminding me of that little fact, Della," she said, yawning again.

"Rest. I'll let the guys know you're taking a nap."

Caro didn't bother trying to open her eyes to tell her friend good-bye. She didn't even hear the other woman leave.

* * * *

"Try this and see if you like it, Caro." Gressen handed her a small plate with something that looked a little like a piece of fried chicken on it.

They'd been plying her with different dishes that were high in iron and protein ever since she'd returned home several days earlier. So far, she liked a little less than half of what they'd put in front of her. She assured them that what they'd found that she liked was plenty to choose from, but they took their job as mates seriously and continued searching for her favorite foods that were good for her.

She sighed and cut off a piece to pop into her mouth. Expecting a crunchy chicken taste, Caro almost choked to find instead a honey flavored barbeque tang that was melt in your mouth delicious.

"Well? What do you think?" Sabin asked from his position in the food prep area.

"This is amazing. It's really good. Add this to the top of my favorite foods list," she said, digging into the rest of the delicious meal.

"That is perfect. We've managed to identify at least eight foods that are high in the iron she needs, while containing the amounts of protein her body will need as well." Sabin started putting away the cooking supplies he'd pulled out and let the automation take over once he'd tidied up what it wouldn't.

"How are you feeling, sweetness?" Gressen asked as he sat next to her.

"Good. I get tired after being up for more than five or six hours, but it will get better soon. Then, once I'm about seven months along, I'll need a nap every day until the baby is born. Of course, the last few weeks I won't be able to get comfortable enough to rest for long, but that's something to worry about later," she said with a straight face.

Caro loved shocking them with the expectations of what it was going to be like for all of them over the next few months. They'd finally determined that she was about six weeks along. That could be plus or minus a week since she'd not had a period since they'd left the Earth's orbit. They'd all worried that they weren't going to be able to have children once they reached their new home. Then when they'd crashed, it hadn't been a top priority to think about.

Well, she bet everyone started thinking about it now that it had been announced that she was "with young." She prayed that everything would go by the book so that there wouldn't be any surprises. She happened to be the first female to have a child in many, many years on this planet, and the only female of their group so far to become pregnant. Caro was a little worried about who would help with the delivery when no one she knew had ever delivered a baby before.

Somehow, the fact that Sabin had studied up on it didn't reassure her much. She wished they could at least find someone who'd been present when a child was born, but no one from her group had participated in an actual delivery in the past either.

While Della had promised to be right by her side during the entire process, Caro wished for someone who'd done this before to help her through it. She'd never tell Della that, but it crossed her mind several times a day.

"I haven't been able to get much training done at all these last few days," Gressen said as Sabin sat down across from them.

"Why not?" Caro asked between bites.

"All the males want to do is discuss the fact that you are going to have the first young on our planet in forty or so odd years. Most of us can't even remember there ever being someone that young in the city."

"Wow! I guess I never thought about how old you might be. I'm twenty-eight based on our Earth's years. How old are the two of you?" Caro was a little scared to find out.

"I'm forty-eight," Sabin told her. "That is young for my people."

"I'm fifty-two. I'm considered to be at the end of my young adulthood." Gressen's matter of fact statement of his age had Caro choking.

"Easy, Caro. What's wrong?" Sabin asked.

"I didn't realize how old you were. Do you realize that you're my father's age? Oh. My. God!" She hadn't even thought about it. They didn't look much older than she did. Another thought hit her but Sabin interrupted her.

"We have much shorter years than you do back on Earth, plus, we seem to live longer than your people do. Our kind usually didn't mate until they were in their thirties and even forties. Their first young were not born until they were in their mid to late forties."

"How old are the elders? To me, they appear to be in their seventies and eighties for the most part," she said with a squeak in her voice.

"Let's see," Gressen said looking up at the ceiling for a few seconds. "I believe that Soku is one hundred fifteen, and Alsure is close to his age at one hundred twelve. I do not know of Aveste's age. We have elders who are over one twenty-five. The few females who are left are at least one hundred and ten, or twelve, but since we have not seen them in many years, I can't recall without asking."

"The last time one of them passed, when it was announced and the city mourned, she'd been one hundred and seven," Sabin told her. "There are only about three, or maybe four, left now."

"That is so sad," Caro said. "I still can't believe how much older you are than I am though."

"Does it change your mind about us, Caro?" Gressen asked in a voice that screamed fear.

"No. It doesn't, Gressen. I still want to be your mate and I still love you both," she told them.

"Love us?" Sabin asked. "I've read much about this emotion humans have, but am still not sure about its meaning. It seems to cover anything from how you feel about your parents or your children, to how you feel about the way your hair looks. It seems a little vague and insulting to be compared to someone's feelings about their hair or even their favorite food."

Caro smiled. She'd never thought about it like that. They did use the word for just about everything, which really didn't make it all that special to say to someone when she really meant that they were the most important person or thing in her life. No wonder she hadn't heard it from either of her mates. To them, it would have been an insult to her.

"You're right. I'm sorry. But I'm not sure how to tell you what I'm feeling now," she admitted.

"I will tell you how we feel about you, sweet Caro." This came from Gressen who normally remained stoic and let Sabin do the talking when it came to anything outside of sex. "You are everything to us. You are our breath, our heartbeat, and our light. Our happiness depends on your smiles and laughter. Having touched you and watched you sleep, after hearing your laugh and tasting your tears, not having you with us would leave us in darkness with no hope left to us."

Caro blinked back tears. Saying she loved them really had been an insult. For a race who showed and experienced very little emotion, Gressen's words, so full of meaning and truth, completely shamed her and thrilled her all at the same time. How could she ever express the depth of her feelings for them after that?

"I—I'm speechless. No one has ever told me, or anyone I know, something as profound and humbling as the words you just gave me. I don't deserve that amount of devotion and feeling," she told Gressen in a husky voice.

Her throat tightened just thinking about it all over again. She had no doubt she would feel the same way in twenty years. If she lived to be a hundred and twenty, Caro doubted she'd ever get over this moment.

"Thank you, Gressen. I will cherish your feelings for the rest of my life." She looked over at where Sabin sat smiling at them both. "Sabin, my heart beats for both of you. You've opened your home to me, fed and clothed me, and sought only to make me happy and comfortable. Each of you hold a piece of my heart and soul. I will never ask for them back because I know they are safer with you than they ever were with me. On top of all of what you have provided for me, you've given me a child to love and watch grow. There are no words for how I feel about you both."

"We will watch over the young together and cherish the new life we've been allowed for our family unit and for our people. Thank you for giving us a new reason to get up each morning." Sabin leaned over and kissed her.

"Our biggest worry will be making sure everyone doesn't spoil the child with attention and gifts," Gressen grumbled.

"I hadn't thought about that. It will be as if the baby has hundreds of uncles and grandparents." Caro grinned. "Life is good."

Veran burst into the common area, his normally bronzed skin pale and clammy looking. Caro immediately knew that something was wrong with Della.

"Veran, what is wrong?" Gressen asked, standing up.

"Della, something is wrong with her. She hasn't stopped losing her stomach for the last hour," he said with a tremble in his voice.

"Is this the first time she's been ill?" Sabin asked as he grabbed his case from the entrance area and hurried back toward Veran's hall with the other male.

"Caro, stay here with Gressen in case what she has is contagious. You cannot afford to become ill."

She smiled and looked at Gressen. "I do believe it is contagious, but she got it from me, not the other way around."

Gressen frowned. "What are you talking about, Caro? How do you know what she has?"

"I bet she is suffering from morning sickness."

"Morning sickness?" Gressen's brows drew tighter in puzzlement. "It's not morning. It's past last meal, Caro."

"Morning sickness is just the term given to it since most females who are pregnant are sick first thing in the morning, but some are sick at different times during the day. Some never really get sick at all, and some are sick all the time."

"That doesn't make sense." He shook his head then slowly looked up at her with wide eyes, the gold surrounding his dark green eyes shown as he realized what she'd said.

"Pregnant? You think she is with young as you are?" he asked with excitement.

"Yes. I bet she is. That means we will be able to help each other and get all emotional together and you, your brother, Veran, and Kane can hover over us not knowing what to do with two sobbing females one moment, and two starving females the next."

"Two females with young in one family unit is going to be a most difficult living arrangement for some time, I suppose." Gressen grinned and pulled her into his arms.

"Just think, Gressen. Our child will have another to play with. They won't be lonely for a playmate, and can learn together and grow up with each other."

"Young, female. They are called young," he told her in mock sternness.

Caro laughed. "Young, child, baby, they're all the same thing for a tiny bundle of joy. I can't wait for Sabin to return so I can see the look on his face when he realizes what is wrong with her."

"Caro, Gressen! You are not going to believe this!" Sabin's excited voice calling down the hall as he all but ran toward them left them both laughing uncontrollably in a heap on the couch.

When Sabin arrived, he slid to a stop and just stared at the two of them. "You already knew, didn't you," he said with a wide smile.

"We already knew. Levasso has the beginnings of a new generation percolating in your family unit. The city will be alive once again, Sabin. Let's go to bed and celebrate," Caro said with what she hoped was a mischievous grin.

Both males reached for her at the same time, making Caro squeal in delight. This was the life she'd dreamed of when she was a teenager. For a long time, she'd believed it to be a fairytale that could never come true. When their Earth began to die because their sun was falling apart, she'd buried that dream for what she thought would be permanent. All it had taken was a wrong turn inside a black hole to find happiness, contentment, and a future well beyond those dreams she'd buried years before.

THE END

WWW.MARLAMONROE.COM

ABOUT THE AUTHOR

Marla Monroe has been writing professionally for about eleven years. Her first book with Siren was published in January of 2011, and she now has over 70 books available with them. She loves to write and spends every spare minute either at the keyboard or reading. She writes everything from sizzling-hot cowboys, emotionally charged BDSM, and dangerously addictive shifters, to science fiction ménages with the occasional badass biker thrown in for good measure.

Marla lives in the southern US and works full-time at a busy hospital. When not writing, she loves to travel, spend time with her cats, and read. She's always eager to try something new and especially enjoys the research for her books. She loves to hear from readers about what they are looking for next in their reading adventures.

You can reach Marla at themarlamonroe@yahoo.com, or
Visit her website at www.marlamonroe.com
Her blog: www.themarlamonroe.blogspot.com
Twitter: @MarlaMonroe1
Facebook: www.facebook.com/marla.monroe.7
Google+: https://plus.google.com/u/0/+marlamonroe7/posts
Goodreads:
https://www.goodreads.com/author/show/4562866.Marla_Monroe
Pinterest: http://www.pinterest.com/marlamonroe/
BookStrand: http://bit.ly/MzcA6I
Amazon page: http://amzn.to/1euRooO

For all titles by Marla Monroe, please visit
www.bookstrand.com/marla-monroe

Siren Publishing, Inc.
www.SirenPublishing.com

Lightning Source UK Ltd.
Milton Keynes UK
UKOW01f0850250917
309824UK00013BA/894/P

9 781682 952375